Maine Character Energy

A Charity Anthology

Edited by Sarah Parke

Maine Character Energy: A Charity Anthology

Published by Rogue Owl Press. First edition. January 2024.
ISBN: 979-8-9873401-6-5

In honor of the victims, survivors, and families of the Lewiston mass shooting that occurred on Wednesday, October 25, 2023.

Contents

Introduction

On October 27, 2023, the *New York Times* published a guest essay by Stephen King titled, "Stephen King on Mass Shootings: We're Out of Things to Say." The King of Horror and born-and-bred Mainer has been a vocal advocate for stricter gun laws for years, and his essay came just two days after the mass shooting in Lewiston, Maine, a community roughly fifty miles from where he grew up. The massacre in Lewiston on October 25, 2023, claimed the lives of eighteen people and wounded thirteen others. It marked the thirty-sixth mass killing of the year in the United States. It was also the deadliest mass shooting in Maine's history.

King's essay conveys his anger and frustration toward our nation's obsession with firearms and the elected officials who offer only empty platitudes and prayers. "There is no solution to the gun problem and little more to write, because Americans are addicted to firearms."

It's the contradiction at the heart of King's diatribe that resonated with me as a writer and editor. Taking the time to put your frustrations into words and sharing those words with an audience, I think, speaks to some degree of hope that perhaps people can be persuaded to take action, to do better. Words have the power to convince, revile, entertain, and charm. Stories hold a unique kind of power. Stories can transcend time and place, making even the most mundane seem magical. When the right words are placed in a specific order, stories can evoke memories, provoke anger or lust, and maybe even provide comfort for a little while.

King's essay was a call to action for me, and this charity anthology, dedicated to the victims, survivors, and families of the Lewiston, Maine, massacre, is the result.

I've never lived in Maine. I'm what locals would call "from away," but I've loved the state for years. I earned my MFA from the University of Southern Maine, and I spent residencies in Freeport and Brunswick. I owe a debt of gratitude to Maine because that's where I found my first writing community. It's one of those rare places where you'll find pocket-sized artist colonies where creative-types spend the long, dark winters honing their craft: writing, sculpting, quilting, carving.

Just a few weeks before the shooting in Lewiston, my husband and I had celebrated our ninth anniversary in Bar Harbor, and I visited Acadia National Park for the first time. No one warned me about the fog. It tucked itself over the island like a flannel sheet and did strange things to my other senses. The morning we hiked around Jordan Pond, the fog was so thick I couldn't see the water or the mountains around us, but the smell of damp leaves and pine sap was stronger, the sounds of scurrying red squirrels and bird song were louder.

I think our country lives within a similar kind of fog that comes from the trauma of near-daily tragedy. We hear the victims' families crying on the news, we can feel the anxiety creeping into our schools and workplaces, but we can't see a way forward.

I wanted to create a story collection that would celebrate the resilient spirit of Mainers. Many of the authors have lived in, or currently reside in, the state. The stories in this collection all take place in Maine, from its rocky beaches to its pine-scented lakes, to the granite-covered mountaintops. Maine also serves as a kind of character, summoning the fog to thwart fishermen and brandishing the Northern Lights to dazzle hikers. You might recognize some familiar Maine archetypes—the widow, the lobsterman, the youth who longs to be anywhere else—but their stories will surprise and captivate you.

The other goal of this collection is to raise money for a national nonprofit organization that is working to end the cycle of gun violence. By purchasing a copy of this anthology, you are helping support Everytown for Gun Safety's* important work: identifying local and national political candidates who support common sense gun safety; registering and educating young voters; amplifying the voices and experiences of survivors, teachers, parents, and gun owners; and more.

I hope you enjoy reading this collection. I was floored by the support I received for this project from the writers in my community, and I hope it serves as proof that words, coupled with action, can heal.

Sarah Parke
December 2023

*For more information on Everytown for Gun Safety, visit everytown.org.

Patchwork

by Shannon Bowring

T he cabin is dusty and smells of decay, hollow animal bones hidden under the rough-hewn floor. Along one wall, a table sits beneath a sun-yellowed window; an icebox stands beside the old cookstove. A stone fireplace takes up most of the center of the room. In one corner is a carved pine bed topped with a Double Wedding Ring quilt in shades of blue and green.

"Did I ever tell you Nana sewed that quilt when she and Pop got married?"

"Don't think you did."

Dean stands with one foot over the threshold of the room and the other planted on the front porch. His brown hair lifts in the breeze.

"Why those colors?" His voice is hesitant, as though he's forgotten how to speak without the usual background noise of their lives—Jenna's irritating pop music, the whir of Leigh-Anne's sewing machine, the low murmur of the nightly news.

"Nana said the blue was for her, because her head was usually in the clouds. But Pop always had his feet on the ground."

"I like it." Dean joins her inside the cabin. His pinkie grazes hers.

"Yeah," says Leigh-Anne. She tucks her hand into her back pocket. "I like it, too."

***

Her great-grandparents built this cabin in the North Maine Woods in the 1800s, cutting, stacking, and chinking every log by hand, and the property has been handed down through generations of Travers ever since. Leigh-Anne's father owns it now; one day she'll share it with her siblings.

She spent many summer days here as a child, sitting on her grandparents' laps with her sticky face buried in their necks, Nana smelling of burnt sugar, Pop of spruce sap and spearmint. Pop taught her to fish and build a fire; Nana revealed the wonders of the cookstove, baking biscuits until every surface of the cabin was covered in a fine layer of flour.

But camp life wasn't all romance. Spiders lurked everywhere, mice chewed on Leigh-Anne's pillow, and if she needed to use the bathroom, she had to slog fifty yards from the cabin to the outhouse. As she and her siblings grew older, the frequent treks to camp stopped all but for one week each summer, when the extended Travers family would smoosh together in the cabin. Everyone smelling of bug spray and lake water; endless games of cribbage. But eventually that ended, too. The past few years, the cabin mostly only gets used by Dean for his annual fall deer-hunting trips with his buddies.

And that was okay with Leigh-Anne, until last week, when she was hit with a gut punch of nostalgia looking through old photo albums. As she brushed her fingers lovingly across her grandparents' faces, memories of camp came rushing back in vivid detail. Echo of loons across the lake. Pop sipping Allen's coffee brandy on the front porch as fireflies flickered. Her brother and sister, sweat-sticky, running barefoot through the bracken.

"We should go up to camp for the weekend," she suggested over the supper table that night. "All three of us."

Jenna, eleven-almost-twelve, stabbed her fork into the pile of scalloped potatoes on her plate. "Too many bugs."

"But don't you remember how much fun you used to have there when you were little? You and your cousins?"

"There's no TV there or anything. No thanks."

"You watch too much TV."

"You and Dad should go without me."

Dean's fingers tightened on his knife as he spread margarine on a piece of bread.

"Never mind," Leigh-Anne said. "It was a silly idea."

Later that night, as she and Dean lay in bed, she tried to concentrate on *The Things They Carried*, which Trudy Haskell had assigned for the library book club. But the words felt as heavy as the soldiers' packs. Those poor men humping through that wasteland. Leigh-Anne's thoughts kept straying to her brother, who served over there for a year before coming back with a missing foot and a haunted look in his eyes that still hasn't gone away, two decades later.

She marked her page with a Dalton Diner receipt (Dean's typical solitary weekday breakfast: one piece of rye toast, scrambled eggs, oatmeal, one cup of coffee, grand total $3.15) and set the book on her nightstand. She snuggled into the pillows and closed her eyes.

"We could go, if you want."

At the sound of her husband's voice, Leigh-Anne opened her eyes and stared up at the popcorn ceiling. She knew without looking that Dean's face was shadowed in the dim lamplight, cheeks hollowed out like those of a starving person.

"Been a long time since we looked in on the place."

"Dad takes good care of the property." She chose her words with the same precision she applied when administering vaccinations at the clinic. "It's not really necessary for us to go."

"Still, might be good to get away. Take a long weekend. Think Richard would give you a few days off?"

She fought the urge to look over at him, afraid that if she did, he would change his mind. Go quiet again. Her stomach started to ache.

"What about Jenna?"

"She can stay over at Aimee's house. I'm sure Tim and Cheryl wouldn't mind."

No, her stomach didn't hurt—it was nerves Leigh-Anne was feeling, nerves she hadn't felt in years.

"That should be all right," she said.

Dean clicked off the lamp and they lay there as warm summer air blew in through the open windows. A familiar silence settled over them like a wool blanket, comforting but also vaguely itchy, uncomfortable.

"So, it's settled," he murmured. "We'll go."

Apart from discussions about Jenna's bad attitude and the leaky water heater, it was the longest conversation she and Dean had had in weeks. What would they talk about for four days in the middle of the woods? The thought kept Leigh-Anne awake long after his snores filled the room.

***

The forest breathes. She can feel it in the air, the subtle inhalations and exhalations of the trees, flutter of wings unseen. Evergreens stretch their limbs toward the sun like dancers reaching for the spotlight. From the tangle of tree branches comes the cacophony of blue jays and chickadees and white-throated sparrows. A cool morning wind blows off the lake, carrying with it the mineral smells of moss, water, an old bait trap left to dry on the dock.

From where she sits on the front porch, Leigh-Anne can just make out Dean's slender silhouette in her father's red canoe, halfway across the lake. Beyond him lie undulating, wooded hillsides that lead all the way to Mount Katahdin, some sixty miles to the south. She imagines Dean tilting his face toward those hills, closing his eyes to absorb the warmth of the sun. Before they were married, he'd talk about taking to the woods, living off the land. With his patience and self-reliance, he would have done well in the wild. But Leigh-Anne liked Dalton, despite spending most of her bored teenage years proclaiming it was the place where dreams went to die. And she wanted kids, a regular job, a steady paycheck. All the things that make up a normal, quiet, happy existence. Sometimes, though, she thinks with an ache about that wilderness life they never led. The losses they wouldn't have had to endure.

Dean paddles back into shore, dismounting gracefully from the tippy canoe, and comes to sit beside her on the porch. He smells like sunshine and sawdust. It occurs to Leigh-Anne that at thirty-five, her husband is just as handsome as when they married fifteen years ago. He's stayed trim. His hair has lightened, but not yet begun to thin. The grief he's carried, ever since they lost their son, has taken away the playfulness he once had, but none of the kindness, or the softness behind his hazel eyes.

"Catch any fish?"

"They must still be sleeping."

Far across the water, a loon cries. Sound of sorrow, echo of lonely.

"Clouds coming in, over to the west." Dean places his hand near hers on the top step. "Prob'ly rain later."

She lets her hand remain where it is. She can feel the warmth from his skin, so close to her own. "Looks that way."

Later, she paddles the canoe out into one of the lake's shallow coves. Within twenty minutes, she catches four trout. With great care not to hurt their pliant, silver bodies, she places each fish back into the water, their iridescent scales flashing in the sun before they escape to the safety of their own dark world.

"Catch anything?" Dean asks when she returns to the cabin.

"Not a damn thing."

***

The rain comes after supper, rolling in with charcoal clouds that swirl above the lake. As darkness gathers in the cabin, Dean lies down to read; Leigh-Anne remains at the table, working on a crossword puzzle under the circle of light cast by a Coleman lantern.

When they were first married, she and Dean would do the *Bangor Daily* crossword every Saturday morning as they lay in bed wrapped in bathrobes. Each weekend felt like an escape to a fancy hotel—orange juice and pancakes on the breakfast tray at the foot of the bed, drowsy ache in her legs after a night of lovemaking. But once Jenna was born, the routine changed—early morning feedings and diaper changes, spilled milk and baby puke all over Leigh-Anne's favorite yellow blanket. And a couple years later, Anthony came along. Weekends were never the same with kids. Nothing was ever the same.

"Hey, Mr. Carpenter. You'd know this." Leigh-Anne raises her voice to be heard over the patter of rain on the tin roof. "What's a resin typically used in cabinetmaking? Eight letters."

"Melamine."

Outside, the wind picks up, tops of pine trees whipping like catapults. She shivers despite the humidity in the air. Dean rises from the bed. As he lifts his flannel over his head, she catches a glimpse of his white t-shirt and flat stomach, a dark strip of hair disappearing into the gingham boxers that peek above his jeans.

"Here," he says. "Warm yourself up."

His callused fingers linger on her wrist as he gives her the shirt. He offers a shy smile and returns to the bed, his book. Leigh-Anne considers lying down next to him, flipping through one of the old *National Geographics* that have sat in a wicker basket near the couch ever since Jenna was a baby. Instead, she deals herself a hand of solitaire. Outside, thunder rolls across the rippled sky.

★★★

The next day is clear and bright. Dean suggests a swim, and Leigh-Anne surprises herself by agreeing. She stands on the weathered dock and strips down to her underwear when he isn't looking. She can't recall the last time he saw her without her clothes on. She's beginning to take on the same unfortunate shape as her mother—slender in her shoulders and breasts, heavy as a water-logged pear in her ass and thighs. Time hasn't been as forgiving with her body as it has for Dean. But then time has been cruel to them both in other ways.

Neither of them has said what they've both been thinking since they opened their eyes as morning sun flooded into the cabin. It's July 20th, his birthday.

Anthony.

Their dark-haired, laughing, bright-eyed boy. He loved rockets, dinosaurs, green apples. And he loved his older sister. From the day he was born, he'd locked eyes with Jenna, wrapped his little fist around her thumb, and that was that. Jenna, two years older, had loved being a big sister, teaching Anthony everything from the rules of dress-up to the places in the pantry where Leigh-Anne stashed her secret rations of chocolate. Their house was small, and the kids had to share a room, but Jenna never complained, even when Anthony's cries woke her in the middle of the night.

But then one February morning when he was three, it was Jenna's screams that brought Leigh-Anne and Dean running into the kids' bedroom.

"It was an accident, Mumma," she sobbed as Dean raced back to the kitchen to call 911. "I know you told us not to jump on the bed, but he wanted to, I couldn't stop him."

Jenna hadn't let them remove Anthony's empty bed from the room for months after the funeral. They'd finally had to sneak it out one day while she was at school, Dean loading the tiny frame and mattress onto his truck with the other trash destined for that day's dump run. Jenna hadn't spoken to them for a week afterward.

Leigh-Anne pulls in a deep breath before cannonballing into the lake. It's cool beneath the surface. Reeds tickle her ankles. Underwater, she finds the pile of rocks her brother built beside the rusting wagon wheels of the dock. She marvels at the fact it still exists, that the shape has held over all these years.

When she surfaces, she swims out a bit, then turns back toward the camp and treads water. Dean is sitting on the edge of the dock. Water drips down his bare arms, bare chest, bare calves. He sees Leigh-Anne looking and lifts one arm in a salutation she knows she isn't obliged to return. She holds her arm up anyway, and they stay like that for several moments, palms lifted toward the sun.

Six years have passed. Today he would have turned nine.

***

They spend the rest of the day outside, clearing brush, tidying up the wood pile. Every few minutes one of them says something mundane—a comment on the weather or the potential cost of a new water heater—and the other responds with polite interest.

Leigh-Anne can't recall the last time they were together like this. When she isn't at the clinic, she spends most of her time cooking, cleaning, or trying to ignore Jenna's loud music and barbed comments. Dean works all day from his carpentry shop in the backyard, only coming inside to eat meals and watch the evening news. It's been this way since Anthony died. They're still relatively young, but she feels so old. So ancient.

"Look."

Leigh-Anne glances up to see Dean holding a baby pinecone toward her.

"It's beautiful."

And it is—but what's even better is the beam of boyish delight on her husband's face.

Dean's thin lips curve upward.

"For you," he says, laying the pinecone in her hand. His thumbnail grazes her palm. Shivers, all the way down.

★★★

They eat supper on the porch—grilled cheese sandwiches, Humpty Dumpty chips, apple slices.

"We used to have this same meal almost every night when we were just starting out," says Dean. "Remember?"

The sun casts a pleasant golden light on his face, and Leigh-Anne looks at him longer than she normally would. She realizes she's never told him she likes the beard he started to wear over the past couple years.

"God," she says, "we were babies back then."

"Glad we have more money now."

"Still not much. But enough."

"Yeah," Dean agrees. "Enough."

When he grins, he looks so much like his twenty-year-old self that Leigh-Anne feels dizzy, as though she's been pushed through the veil of time back to their shag-carpeted trailer on Linden Avenue. She can almost hear the pop and scratch of the needle on their old turntable, John Denver's reedy, comforting voice.

In the middle of the night, she wakes to the sound of an owl hooting outside. Dean has fallen asleep with the lantern on; its weak battery glow illuminates his face and a corner of her grandmother's quilt. Holding her breath, Leigh-Anne reaches out one slim hand. His beard is softer than she imagined. In his sleep, he rolls toward her. She lies awake. Listens to him breathe. Inches her foot toward his shin. His skin is warm against her toes, and his eyelids flutter in time with her rapid heartbeat. She remembers how he used to whisper her name as they moved together in the darkness of their bedroom—slowly, with the same kind of reverence he used for the names of all his favorite trees.

***

They swim again the next day, floating side-by-side in the water. Afterward, they sit beside the lake. Dean tells her about his current project, a standup wardrobe for Arlene Nadeau. Leigh-Anne shares her concerns about Jenna's new obsession with makeup—"Do we tell her she looks like a drunk clown?"

The heat rises as the sun moves across the sky. Dean makes gin and tonics, which they sip as they recline in the Adirondack chairs Pop made decades ago. Any silence that falls between them is filled with forest sounds. Swishing pines, persistent knock of a woodpecker, gentle lapping of waves on pebbled shore—a natural placeholder until one of them thinks of something else to say. It's the most they've talked in years. Leigh-Anne's belly darts with gin and butterflies. She's terrified to ruin the spell, afraid of saying something that will push Dean back into his familiar silence.

"Want to tell you something."

She looks at him, sitting there in his blue swimming trunks and faded Dalton Bodacious Brass Band t-shirt. He twirls his thumb around the rim of his glass. Circle, circle, circle.

"I started taking this medicine," he says. Voice no louder than the soft breeze off the lake. "Supposed to help with those funks

I get into. Don't really know how it works. But I think it is. Working, I mean."

About a month ago, she'd seen the pills in the cupboard where Dean keeps his coffee, tucked behind a fingerpainted *I LUV U DADDY* mug. She knew it was there so she wouldn't find it—she's stayed away from caffeine since she was pregnant with Jenna. Even reading his name over and over on the orange bottle, she couldn't believe it. Prozac. Prescribed by Dr. Haskell. Leigh-Anne wasn't surprised Richard hadn't told her about the medicine—that would've gone against all sorts of health codes. No, she was surprised because up until then, Dean had refused any kind of medical intervention to combat the depression that had plagued him since Anthony died. Wouldn't even consider it after Leigh-Anne started taking the same meds a couple years back. She wondered what had changed for him. She decided not to ask. Dean's like a cat—approach too fast, he'll run away. Hang back, feign ambivalence, and he might saunter up at his own pace.

Even now, she must measure her response carefully.

"Oh," she says, taking a slow sip of gin. "Damn things made me constipated at first. You?"

He lets out a soft laugh. "Oh, yeah."

Tiny slivers of ice in his glass tinkle as he continues twirling his thumb around the rim. Circle. Circle. Circle.

"But it's good," he finally says. "I think."

"I think so, too."

She reigns in her desire to fling her arms around his neck.

When their stomachs start to rumble, he lays a hand on her arm before she can rise from her chair.

"Let me," he says. "Don't come till I tell you."

While he's gone, Leigh-Anne's thoughts drift to Jenna. She wonders what their daughter is doing right now. Lying in Aimee Fortin's bedroom, probably, reading *Teen Beat*. New Kids on the Block in the background, smell of cinnamon wafting from the kitchen as Cheryl takes a tray of snickerdoodles from the oven. The last time Leigh-Anne picked up Jenna from the Fortins', she'd been struck speechless by how happy her daughter looked. Smiling and thanking Cheryl and Tim for supper, waving goodbye to Aimee and Greg and Sarah. And then as soon as Jenna was in the car, the scowl and the silence was back. Not one word, even when Leigh-Anne offered to take her down to the Shanty for a black raspberry milkshake.

How do you get over something like that? They'll never be the same. You can't blame the kid—shoulda kept a closer eye on things, don't you think?

Leigh-Anne's overheard all the comments around town, carried them like a bundle of kindling strapped to her back over the past six years until she feels her spine might burst into a thousand slivers. And she knows Dean's toiled under his own burden, keeping silent in his effort to keep her or Jenna from feeling any more pain.

When he appears at her side with a checked dish rag slung over his shoulder, Leigh-Anne reaches up to place one hand on his arm. For a few moments, they stay like that, looking into one another's eyes without a word, grief humming through them like an electric current.

Maybe this is the start of something. A new kind of silence, a new way to carry the weight. Never setting it down completely—that would be impossible—but learning how to take it up together.

"Okay." Dean's voice is soft. "I'm ready for you now."

Her breath catches in her throat when she steps into the cabin. On the table, he has laid out spaghetti and meatballs, garlic bread, salad, a bottle of merlot.

"How did you—"

"I snuck all the supplies into the car before we left town. Hid them in the back of the icebox."

Leigh-Anne's heart begins to race as saliva fills the back of her mouth. Heat rises to her cheeks and a darting sensation flits through her stomach—not gin this time, and not only nerves, but something so much more. Desire. How long since she last felt this way? How long since he's put forth any effort to *make* her feel this way?

She knows a lot of couples get divorced after the death of a child. That had never been a thought for either her or Dean—the love they fell into when they were seventeen is still there, despite the silence that has both separated and united them over the years. But any hope of romance disappeared as soon as Anthony jumped off that bed. They've remained mostly celibate since he died. At first it was because Leigh-Anne, who couldn't tolerate birth control, feared getting pregnant. They tried to get back to their once-regular routine after Dean had a vasectomy four years ago. But it was clumsy and robotic, robbed of the passion they once took for granted. Since then, a few times a year, one of them will initiate sex, but it always feels like they're virgins pawing at one another with no idea what to do, and no enthusiasm to figure it out. She can't remember the last time they kissed, let alone attempted anything else—last fall, maybe, as leaves dropped like discarded wishes onto the frosty ground.

"Do you like it?" asks Dean, gesturing to the table.

"I have to sit down."

The wine softens the edges of the spruce-scented night. All the windows are open, insects smacking into the metal screens. She remembers how excited Anthony got that first time she took him into the backyard to show him fireflies. How his eyes sparked in the flicker of all those tiny lights.

"Anthony was happy," Leigh-Anne says. "Wasn't he?"

"He was."

Silence falls between them again—an active, alive silence. She waits, giving Dean time to collect his thoughts.

"I worry about Jenna," he says. "After all this time, she still blames herself."

Leigh-Anne thinks of the relief she feels whenever their daughter leaves the house to go to school or to hang out with Aimee. And then the belly-sick worry she feels each time Jenna gets home even five minutes later than she'd said she would.

Dean takes her hand between both of his. His skin is warm and dry, fingers callused from decades spent crafting beautiful furniture from plain blocks of wood.

"You can say it, Leigh."

"Sometimes I *do* blame her."

There it is, the confession she swore she'd never speak aloud. And then she lets herself cry as more words fall from her mouth, a torrent of words after all these years of silent, solitary suffering.

"She knew he wasn't supposed to jump on the bed. She knew and she let him do it, anyway. I know it's not her fault, but sometimes I think there's a part of me that might never forgive her. And she can *feel* that, I know she can."

Dean doesn't say anything, just sits there holding her hand. After a while, Leigh-Anne's sobs fade, and she opens her eyes to see him gazing at her as tears streak down his face and cling to his beard.

"You've really never blamed her?"

His grip tightens on hers. "I've only ever blamed myself," he says. "For everything."

★★★

They turn off the lanterns and slip beneath the quilt her Nana made so many lifetimes ago—interlocking rings, two souls bound together by a common story. Leigh-Anne curls against Dean's chest and buries her face in his stubbly neck, inhaling his smell of lake water and wood shavings. He twirls her hair around his fingers, and they both laugh when his thumbnail catches on the back of her amethyst post earring. Her heart thunders beneath her nightgown as he presses his warm mouth on hers, his wine-stained tongue flitting between her lips.

Across the moonlit lake, a splash of water is answered by the last of the season's loons. Lifelong mates and their new offspring take up a wild, haunting call, the sound of their efforts echoing from cove to cove, up to the starry sky, as Leigh-Anne pulls her husband closer—closer still.

Can't Get Theah from Heah

by Paul Carro

William Fournier may not have been one of the youngest snowbirds to have ever left Maine for Florida, but he would have been close, having done so at age eight. It was a divorce that did it. His dad got the house in Maine and William got the stuffy new stepfather and the high-rise condo in Florida. It was not an awful life there in Florida, but it was, ironically, given the weather, cold. At forty-five, William had returned to the state for the first time in many years. Visits with his father were few and grew fewer, the more both aged.

Now considered a native of Florida, the man trudged through the Maine forest. Though William started out on a trail, he had lost it some time ago. Thankfully, he knew roughly the direction of the lake, but the GPS on his cellphone had crapped out almost as soon as he entered the woods. Packed with people in August, William sought a remote, quiet area of the lake, one without a commercial beach. That meant rough going, made even rougher because he had not trounced through the woods in so long.

Every time he began appreciating the stunning view, a branch would catch his fishing pole, or bump his tackle box, eliciting curses that drew his attention away from the scenery. He also carried a Thermos strapped to his belt with a carabiner, and it banged relentlessly against his side, interrupting the forest's quiet. Mosquitos were relentless, but their presence meant water was nearby. A break in the trees ahead confirmed it. The lake came into view. A beautiful sight, one of the biggest things he missed about Maine. (His father used to take him to Dundee or Sebago Lake when he was a kid.)

Many of the lakes were so vast that one could not see to the other side, and the blue water fed straight into the sunny sky. In that space between water and sky, it was as if only peace existed, no troubles, no worries, no sorrow. He wished he could pocket it and take it home because life elsewhere was hard. He trudged through the last of the underbrush and walked from the loam onto the sand. It was then that he saw the old man.

"Shit," William said under his breath.

The man sat in a lawn chair, the cheap aluminum frame style with the tattered cross-thatched webbing. An open beer sat atop one armrest. The man wore a Boston Red Sox cap and had a line in the water. The man's tackle box (larger than William's) sat on one side of the lawn chair, a mini cooler on the other. He was somewhere between sixty and a hundred. It was hard to tell. *Mainers were good stock*, William's dad used to say.

"Thought you'd have the place to yourself?" the man said, without ever looking back.

"What?" William called out.

"Proper term is 'shit on a shingle.' Not all old people are deaf, you know," the man said.

William turned red, embarrassed. "I did not mean to suggest anything of the sort."

"An out of towner. You going to make me get up, or you going to come over here for introductions?"

William trudged over and stepped in front of the man. "How did you know I was a tourist?"

"The way you speak to begin, but now that I get a look at you, it's a mite more obvious."

William checked himself. He wondered if he could get away with arguing he was a Mainer, that his father was a lifelong Mainer, but William heard the man out. "Okay, I bite. How so?"

"First off, a man your age with such a cheap rod? And the shoes."

"What about them?"

"The fact you're wearing them. And that they cost more than your rod. Tackle box is no better than what a high schooler might carry. Someone who thinks you only need one lure. And they are new, never used."

Though accurate so far, William suddenly felt bad about the purchase of the fishing rod and tackle box. He had money, he should have done better, bought something higher end. But he had not been fishing since he was a kid and the items in his hands reminded him of those days. William was an adult and could have purchased better equipment. "Is there more?"

"Ayuh. You keep checking your cellphone like it is gonna magically come to life. Locals know there ain't no signal out this far, nor should there be. And you're accompanied by a mosquito band. Listen closely and their buzzing resembles a Waylon tune. Locals have the sense to wear repellant. Natural or store-bought stuff. Beer?" The man reached into the cooler and pulled out a bottle.

"No, thank you."

"Ayuh, one more ingredient in the clue sandwich. Locals bring beer when they fish. Soder for the kids. A Moxie maybe? Didn't bring any but didn't rightly expect a young whippersnapper in my presence. Which leads to my last clue."

"Which is?"

"Locals know this is my fishing spot."

"You got me, pops," William said.

"I'm wicked smaht," the man said. "But didn't need to be with you. No beer but a Thermos. Let me guess. A large—excuse me, venti—coffee of some sort full of mostly sugar."

William had almost forgotten about his Thermos. He simply nodded to the man. The man's line went taut. The man rose to his feet and tugged, trying to snap the hook into flesh. His age showed in how long it took him to get to his feet. Not fast enough. The line pulled free. The fisherman reeled the line in and found a wormless hook.

"Someone is smahta than humans, it seems." The fisherman wormed another hook and then cast it out.

William watched the man for pointers, trying to remember if he even knew how to cast a line. He eyed the coastline. It was a small stretch of beach. Forest claimed the water's edge on either side in both directions. Strange how some lakeside land formed open beaches (filled with beachgoers, boaters, and partiers) while others abutted thick forest.

The man remained standing. He fluffed his line, trying to draw attention to the fresh food in the water. "Can't stop ya from fishin' alongside me, but wouldn't recommend it. Fish catch on fast. A buffet gives them pause. Besides, a few more beers and I become a fart machine."

William laughed, suddenly eight again and enjoying fart jokes. He had forgotten how honest people in Maine were. "No, I was hoping for some privacy."

"Get away from the city? I understand. One hour in Portland or Freeport and I'm ready to get back home. Too much traffic."

William thought of how he saw almost none on his way into the woods. That alone had calmed him, made him miss his old home state a bit. Life was fast elsewhere. Even if there were things worth looking at, there was no time to look at them. The view of the lake was all he needed, but without the conversation, as nice as the man was.

"You look lost," the man said.

"You're very insightful."

"I'm old. Don't get this far without seeing things in people. Tell you what. I know a spot, a secret one. Fish bite all day long. No one knows about it but me. Was going to will the spot to my nephew who fishes, but he has beat me in cribbage so often that I don't want to reward the bastard. Thought I might take the spot to my grave, but you look like you need all the help you can get."

City living caution kicked in for William. He squinted as the fisherman partially vanished in the sun. "If it's so good, then why aren't you fishing there?"

"I'm eighty and one knee ain't so good anymore. Place is difficult to get to, but worth the trip. And I promise no one will be there. You'll have the spot to yourself. Never had no city slicker sneak up on me there."

William looked in both directions. "Which way?"

"Can't get theah from heah," the fisherman said.

"What did you say?" William asked.

"Can't get theah from heah. Need to drive south exactly one quarter mile. The road rises from the water. You'll see a wide pull off. You can park theah and walk. The forest will have a steep drop, which is what my knee can't handle. No trail. When you get near the water, look out for the rough bushes. They bite. I staged some pieces of clothing on the way to suggest it's not worth the trip. Tore up a New York Yankees jersey into strips. Once you get through the brush, you will find a tiny beachhead. Toss your line and say hello to the fish. You're welcome."

The man dropped into his chair. William thanked the man and trudged back to his car. That alone was taxing, and he worried how hard it would be to find the spot. But one quarter mile down the road, William parked and climbed down the steep hill. It was treacherous and loam-filled, so his shoes kept slipping, but he remained on his feet.

Once at the bottom of the hill, he saw the NY logo on a strip of shirt, just like the man said. He yelped in pain while navigating through the pricker bushes' tight branches. He led with the tackle box raised, but it did not keep him from getting pricked left and right.

Mosquitos had vanished, likely knowing there was never any food in the area. For that he was grateful because he dripped blood from various limbs where the bushes scraped him and punctured him good. Finally, William found the clearing. A little oasis on the beach. He stood there and took in the view. It was perfect. Maine was beautiful when he was a kid. It remained so as an adult.

A timeless place. His father considered it heaven. That's why he never left.

William set the tackle and pole down, then scoured the area for rocks. Finding three sizable ones that served his needs, William assembled them at his feet, then picked up the rod. He attached a lure and got a few more punctures from the hook to go with those from the bushes. Once finished, he cast the line, which arced high and far. He had not forgotten how. He possessed more strength than when he was a kid, and it was like a bike. Maybe it was the reminder after watching the old man, or maybe it was his father's lessons.

His dad used to stand behind him when he was a kid and direct William's arm. So awkward at eight that he could have hooked his father, William didn't understand until he got older how dangerous it had been, or how brave his father had been for guiding his arm. With the line out in the water, William bent and stuck the pole in the sand. Then he placed the rocks on all sides so that the fishing pole remained in place. He tugged on the line to make sure a fish's bite would not tip it over. Now he could fish without holding the pole.

William lifted the top tray out of the tackle box and removed a bottle of beer. While the old fisherman had been dead-on with most things, he was wrong about a couple. William opened the bottle of beer and set it down near the pole.

That left the Thermos. The other thing the fisherman had been wrong about. William unscrewed the top and upturned the Thermos. A smaller metal tube fell into his hands. He dropped the useless Thermos to the ground. Affixed to the tube was a strip of masking tape on which was printed a name and date. The name read "Al Fournier," and the date was that of his dad's recent death. The tube contained his father's ashes.

William had tried and failed to find the exact spot his father used to take him fishing. Time eroded some memories and cemented others. He remembered his father guiding his arm, teaching him how to cast, but the spot where they stood could have been anywhere in the state. They talked occasionally on the phone over the years, William and his father, but visits were few. Mostly they talked about fishing together again someday. That never happened.

His mother could not be bothered to make the trip, but there were Maine faces aplenty at the funeral. Kind people, some who knew Al, and some who knew him in passing. That was how Mainers were. They came together to battle grief. There were cucumber and mayonnaise sandwiches, baked beans, red hot dogs, and other fixings at the funeral arranged by some distant relative while William made his way home.

His father had died alone, and it saddened William to think his father had felt pain in the end, but without an autopsy, the exact cause of death was uncertain. William hoped he went in his sleep. Death was a fickle thing that came and went on its own terms. William could only hope it was quick for his father.

William's nana had passed when he was seven. It was his father who consoled him at the funeral. Unable to understand why she had to go, his father had taken him by the shoulders and bent to one knee. He looked into William's crying eyes.

"They're not gone. Not really. People are never gone. If you know where they were and where they went, then you can be their voice. You can remind the world who they were. If you do that, they will always be around. They just knock on your door less is all," his father said.

That started William crying, and he appreciated his father pulling him into a hug. His dad held him until William gathered enough strength to promise he would keep their nana alive. When William asked where heaven was, his father spread his arms wide, gesturing at the beautiful scenery around them.

"You can't get theah from heah, son," he said, meaning the surrounding cemetery, beautiful, as all things Maine were. "You can only get theah from heah." His father touched William's chest over the boy's breaking heart.

When the fisherman had repeated the saying, the sun had hit the man just so, and for a moment it was no longer the fisherman standing there. It was his father, glowing in a halo of sun, young again, smiling down at his boy. His father, holding a fishing pole, letting William know things would be alright.

William opened the canister and spread the ashes in his father's new fishing spot, a place where the fish would always bite, and the beer would always remain cold. William knew where his father was and knew where he had been. He vowed to return with his own pole and fish alongside his father every year. At least once, maybe more often. After all, it was his job to keep his father's memory alive. It comforted William to know his dad was with Nana.

He made his way back through the brush. If the pricker bushes bit, he did not feel them. He drove away from his father's fishing spot, happy to have known the man, and proud to call him his father. He left the sadness behind as well, along with the beauty of the lake. There was no reason for sorrow any longer. He vowed to return home to Maine often. William left with the knowledge he would fish with his father soon.

Glass Eels

by sid sibo

E ven darker than the clouded night, fresh pavement stretches in front of him, the northland's pervasive balsam scent indiscernible above a tarry stink. Fresh tires on the new-to-him pickup hum over unblemished road. Frank revels in speed made smooth by the heavy roller he operates on the construction job, prepping Maine for its summer hordes of RVs and outta-state ragtops. Fast and fabulous, he races toward Bucksport and the weighted fyke net he set earlier. A couple of five-gallon buckets of glass eels and this truck is paid for, counting the lift kit, light bar, and paint job.

He laughs and speeds and the rush at the top of a small rise makes him laugh more. The window opens a world of muscled air against his ears. Like storm-driven swells shattering against splintered coastal rock, this wind roars. He's headed for the Atlantic, following gravity and the Penobscot River, but the translucent eels are lifted by a soundless tidal flow pushing them upstream, freshwater their goal. They'll make it if they can get beyond Brewer, where he bunks with three guys from high school. But at these prices, everyone who needs money is setting nets. Pretty much—everybody.

Like whoever's driving that car ahead. No one else likely to be wandering around in the hours after the bars close, except folks watching tide tables. His lights illuminate arms and more arms in the rear window of the stubby car, making him think *giant spider*. Closer now, he recognizes the mismatched metal of its rear end, and the clouded left taillight. New flagger on the construction crew drives a classic Rez car, from Indian Island. Frank whips left and streaks past, yelling. "Sucks to be slow!" His revving engine swallows the words like it swallows miles, without tasting them. Arms stick out every window of the rusty Olds Ciera, waving. Squashable spider. Wind crawls down Frank's neck and he shivers.

A small bridge crosses a minor tributary stream, overgrown farm fields on both sides of the road, gray and empty. The sound changes first. Then the truck lurches, pulls and drags, fights him, uninterested in the road, wanting to plant itself instead. Skidding, spinning, he wrestles to stay upright. They both win, truck sown in spring mud up to its bumpers, and lightbar still facing a starless sky. Fast, and furious, he's out the door. Shards and shrapnel trash the asphalt between the bridge's low guard rails, and his lights pick out blue paint scrapes from whatever wrecked here earlier. Smoke-tinted glass crunches under his boots, and he kicks it out of his way. The lone tire that landed on the road hisses out its last air. The sound that makes him cuss loudest, though, is the grunting rumble of an approaching car.

Furious, fast, he pops down his tailgate and drags the spare to the ground. He stands it upright, but under only its own weight the rim is just the width of a 10-ply away from the road.

The spider car rolls to a stop beside him. Forearms leaning all casual on the steering wheel, the flagger looks out his window. "Flatter 'n a flounder, both of 'em."

Frank fumes, silent. State the obvious, shithead.

"We'd give you a lift, but…" Shithead looks behind him at the packed backseat.

Counting kids in the dark isn't possible. On the front passenger side, Frank sees two skinny ones squished together, twinned braids overlapping. As the car pulls forward, his lightbar glitters their black hair into glassy white, sleek and eel-like. Again, arms extend from all sides. Waving.

Frank heaves the useless spare into the ditch. *Dammit-all-to-hell.* Someone's going to poach his nets when they see he isn't there.

He stares at the water. The brook runs over its rocks like fingers on a keyboard, covering his percussive swearing, not that he cares. One sound or the other deafens him, but white backup lights over the blank-eyed stream alert him to the other car's reversal.

"April Fool's!" A rock band of mis-matched voices echoes, bouncing around the bridge. A door opens. Kids stack high beside him, but two crash on Frank's lap as soon as the flagger drops the car in gear. The ones in front straddle buckets and wooden-handled dip nets. Yep. Going elvin'.

No one asks his name, but he learns a few of theirs from the excited squabbles and accusations flying out the windows. Danny. Henry. Rika. Nell. He has no clue which names go with which poking or pummeling hands. The loudest kid sports gel-spiked hair, but he can't tell—boy or girl. He squirms away from tickling fingers when they're turning off the highway, so is stuck trying to sleuth out where they're driving. He can smell white pines, no matter how black their stretching silhouettes. A salty tang in the reversing river.

With a flourish reminding Frank of his stalled-out truck, the flagger spins the car off the muddy two-track, and four doors flip open. He is stiff now, and slow.

"C'mon!" Someone tosses a dip net in his direction.

Gale, he remembers. The flagger's name. He bends to pick up the wooden handle.

Kids scramble through leafless briars, and with stifled yelps they drop off banks into the stream, not a set of rubber waders among them. Frank tests for thorns before balancing his descent with a branch, and damp remnants of spider web stick to his hand. He eases into winter-cold water. Near the surface, baby eels trace back an ancient journey. Voices seem hushed, though not out of a need to keep from spooking the elvers. Swaying spaghetti-like ghosts swim upstream, indomitable, certain. Frank has never dipped before, but from his peripheral vision he watches Gale's steady style. They'll never score as many as what's trapped in his fyke, downriver.

The two smallest kids don't even have nets. Like herons they stalk, poised on one leg in the pulling current, then slice a hand through the reflective surface to lift one elver at a time. Frank can't decipher the strange words of their banter, their amazement. When a baby eel slips back into the river and wriggles on, they grin.

A Star Near Orion

by Bruce Pratt

M y daughter, Nell, gave me a telescope for helping put her through her PhD in astronomy, and to remember her late mother and my wife, Ann. She presented it to me at her post thesis defense party, along with a series of DVDs on how to explore the night sky. Ann loved to lie in the hammock on the deck with Nell and point out stars and constellations, and when the Northern Lights splashed across the heavens, Ann would wake Nell up to show them to her. Nell, who was thirteen when Ann died, inherited her mom's logic and brains so when she declared at fifteen that she'd be an astronomer, I had no doubt she would.

I placed the scope in the bay window that looks across our far fields and a time or two, when I couldn't sleep that summer, took it out to the deck and peered into the night sky. I studied the DVDs and experimented with the different eyepieces and lenses, but never saw anything remarkable, until Nell came home for the long Columbus Day weekend, and showed me how to focus it by aiming at a star she'd had named for her mother in one of those registries you hear advertised on the radio. "Mom loved being out here on fall evenings, so I chose a star near Orion you'll be able to find with the naked eye," Nell said. "You won't see it in the summer, because you turn in before it's dark enough, but I figured you wouldn't be stargazing then anyway."

With Nell's training, the charts and the planisphere she gave me, and by re-watching the DVDs several times, I learned to locate and focus on certain stars and their constellations but always swung back to the star Nell named for Annie, whom I'd loved for more than thirty years.

I also enjoyed surveying my fields, woods, pond, and stream that lie across the road with the telescope, honing in on birds and animals, amazed by the minute details I'd see. In the last pale light of summer evenings, when I've focused the scope on the pond, I've watched ripples from trout rising to a late hatch. I'm red/green colorblind, which, I believe, is why I have developed an acute sense of movement and can often see what is camouflaged to others. When Ann, Nell, and I hiked or canoed, I'd be the first to spot wildlife. Once I watched a pair of otters sliding up and down a bank for several minutes before either of them could detect their dark bodies against the mud. My vision is better than twenty-twenty in both eyes, and I loved wing shooting but haven't been out since I had to put Caleb, the last of my Pointers, down.

One morning last October, I trained the scope on a stand of maple and birch trees three hundred yards or so from the house near a clearing where deer often browse and spied a small tent. Though I allow locals to hunt on my property, it's posted, and anyone who came into the field in the daylight from the road would see the signs.

I took my binoculars from the peg beside the window and focused them on the tent. A moment later the flap flew open, and a dog danced out, followed a few seconds later by a woman wrapped in a blanket. The dog lifted its leg on one of the birches as the woman squatted behind the largest of the maples. The woman appeared tall at that distance and wore a long braid that shone in the early sunlight. She was no one I knew. Holding the blanket around her, she leaned back into the tent and brought out a small bowl, which she dipped in the pond. As she returned to her tent, the blanket parted behind her, revealing long legs. Dead, dew-drenched grass clung to her feet and ankles, as she leaned over and placed the bowl in front of the dog, then gathered the blanket around her. She reached into the tent and produced another bowl into which the dog shoved its snout. While the dog ate, the woman slipped back into the tent.

When she reappeared, she was wearing a baseball cap, hiking shorts, and a long-sleeved shirt. She dragged a large backpack from the tent, then broke the tent down and stuffed it into a bag which she tied to the top of the pack. She leaned against a birch and wiped the grass from her feet before pulling on socks and hiking boots. As I watched her lace her boots, I wondered how she ended up in my field, miles from the nearest hiking trail or major highway. Back Carrabago Road used to be part of a numbered road, County Route Sixty-Nine, but twenty years ago, the state rerouted and renamed it so kids would stop stealing the signs.

The woman rose, hoisted her pack, and leashed the dog. I laid the binoculars on the table and watched them cross the field toward the road. As it was Friday, I decided to tote my returnable bottles down to the road for Red to pick up, as a pretense for speaking to the woman.

The dog sensed me before the woman saw me, barking and wagging its tail, and tugging at the leash when they were still fifty yards away. As I set the red plastic recycling bin down at the road's edge, I heard the woman say, "Ramona, heel," and looked up to see the dog, a chocolate Lab, stop and sit beside the woman who patted her head. As I feigned peering into my mailbox, the woman said, "Good morning."

I turned to face her and said, "And a fine one it is," as she and the dog scrambled up the bank to the edge of the pavement, "though it must've been a tad chilly last night."

"My buddy keeps me warm, and I have a good sleeping bag," the woman said, shielding her eyes against the glare of the sun. "I hope you'll forgive the trespass."

I smiled and said, "No problem, but I did wonder why anyone would be hiking this way."

"That would take a while," the woman said.

Her face and legs were tanned. She had denim-blue eyes ringed by tiny crow's feet and ashy blonde hair. I crossed the road, extended my hand, and said, "Adam Godreau."

Her shake was firm. "Monica Mays," she said, "and this is Ramona."

I knelt next to Ramona who was sitting at Monica's side and rubbed her head. "Aren't you a fine dog," I said. "Would you and Monica like to come up to the house for coffee or a little breakfast?"

"That's kind of you," Monica said, "but I try not to impose on people who've already offered me a kindness."

"No imposition," I said. "Your camping in the field wasn't any kindness on my part."

Monica stared at me for several seconds then said, "Coffee would be very nice, thank you."

As we climbed up the driveway, Monica kept peering over her shoulder, as if she was checking to see if she was being followed, but when she said, "You have an extraordinary view," I realized that she was seeing the valley for the first time in a way I see it every day.

"Never tired of it in twenty-five years," I said. Then I pointed at the house and said, "When my wife, Ann, was alive she'd stand in front of the big window on a nice morning in any season and say, 'Just another ugly day in paradise, eh Adam?'"

"You live here alone?" Monica asked.

"I do now. Though my daughter, Nell, who's a postdoc at MIT, is coming up next weekend. I missed her while she was getting her PhD at Stanford so I'm grateful she's back on the East Coast."

"What kind of work do you do?" Monica asked as we reached the dooryard.

"I retired from the Department of Natural Resources and opened a consulting business. I advise woodlot owners on best practices, but most days I'm content to putter around the farm and enjoy my woods and fields."

Inside the house, Monica took off her pack and sat at the table in front of the big window, while I made coffee. "I haven't eaten yet, may I offer you breakfast?" I asked.

"Sounds great," Monica said. "I'd appreciate whatever you're having."

I lit the flame under bacon, began boiling water for the oats, ground beans for the press, and said, "How do you take your coffee?"

"Black, please," Monica said.

When all I had left to do was watch the bacon and stir the oatmeal, I said, "You said it would take a while to explain why you're out here on Back Carrabago Road. Don't feel obligated to tell me, but I am interested."

Monica glanced up and said, "Even the abridged version is complicated."

"My morning is free," I said.

"But Ramona and I do need to get going soon," she said.

"I can give you a lift if you'd like."

"But you won't know where I'm going," Monica said, "until I tell you how I got here."

I brought the food and the coffee press to the table, got the maple syrup and milk from the refrigerator, and sat down across from Monica. I set a mug of coffee at her place then handed her a bowl of oatmeal and a plate with three slices of bacon.

Monica blew across her coffee and said, "There is nothing sweeter than real syrup. Is this from the farm?"

I nodded, my mouth full of oatmeal. "I have a four-acre sugarbush up above here, so I can rotate taps and still have syrup for the year."

Monica sipped her coffee, ate a piece of bacon and some oatmeal, wiped her mouth, and said, "A year ago, I was thirty pounds heavier, taking medications for high cholesterol and anxiety, and working seventy hours a week in my private law practice, doing everything from DWI cases, to wills, divorces, and real estate closings. My ex-husband, Larry, was also spending long hours at his office, not working, but romancing his college girlfriend, Lucinda, who'd landed back in our town after ten years working as a well-paid model on the West Coast. The short version is I walked in on them, he said it wasn't what I thought, think of the kids—they're both in college—we all make mistakes, we can start over, all the clichés from movies and books. I crashed." Monica paused to take a bite of bacon and said, "I sent Larry packing and rescued Ramona, who the Humane Society workers said, liked walks. I discovered I did as well. I squeezed Larry as dry as I could, finished up all my cases and decided to take a year off. I sold our house in Chatboro, New York, sent Larry his share, and set out to see the world on foot. I've been hiking around New England. The longest stretch I've done was three weeks last May and June, mostly in Vermont. When I get tired of traipsing around, I get a motel, if I can find one that will accept Ramona, or rent a car and drive back to Chatboro. Later, when it gets too cold for us to camp and tramp, I'll start up my practice again."

Monica paused to eat some more oatmeal and the rest of her bacon. "This is a true treat," she said. "I eat a lot of freeze-dried hiker's food. If I didn't have Ramona, I'd eat at restaurants, but she protects me and keeps me company." At the sound of her name, Ramona nuzzled Monica's leg. "Don't you girl?" Monica asked.

"Lots of people claim they'd love to do what you're doing," I said, "but most would give up in no time."

"The way I see it," Monica said, "walking is better than therapy or Valium."

"If I may ask, how did you end up on Back Carrabago Road?"

"I started out last week down the coast. I hiked from campground to campground, some private, some state owned, with the intention of getting to Ragged Head."

"Any particular reason?" I asked.

"The answer to that is a qualified 'yes'," Monica said. She drank the last of her coffee and when I held up the press to see if she'd like more, she said, "Half a cup would be great."

Monica sipped her coffee and said, "For years I heard gossip about a distant relative who'd been shunned by our extended family, and who, another rumor insisted, lived as a recluse on a farm near Ragged Head where her parents had been banished for some social impropriety." Monica paused as if to recall a detail then said, "One day when I was luxuriating in self-pity, I contacted a private investigator who'd done work for me and told him what little I knew about this woman. A few weeks ago, when I was home, he told me that with the help of a genealogist he discovered the woman's name, but that she had died last spring. I have friends with ties to Ragged Head, some summer people, some emigrants who still have relatives in the area. Not one knew the woman. That piqued my interest and spurred me to come up here. I'd expected to make Ragged Head yesterday, but misjudged the time it would take. It was dusk when I set up camp," Monica said, "and I gambled on the posted signs being for hunters."

"Who was your relative?"

"Addie Alberts."

My face must have betrayed me. Monica said, "Is that shock or disgust?"

"No offense," I said, "but it's hard to believe no one admitted to at least recognizing her name. She was infamous, and, I'm afraid, a generally unpleasant person."

Monica smiled and said, "No offense taken. In fact, I'm more intrigued by Addie now that I've met someone who can confirm she existed."

I stared a moment into my coffee and said, "I didn't know Addie well at all. Old Timers insist she was a nice kid, who, after her parents died, became spiteful and mean-spirited, more hostile, and combative each year."

"I wish someone in the family had told me the details about Addie's parents' banishment," Monica said, "but maybe I'll intuit something at the farm."

"The farm is a stunning property, but it's a long way up there and it'd be best if I drove you," I said. "Addie willed it to The Humane Society—just like her to favor animals over people—and they've been sprucing it up to put on the market next spring. It'll fetch half a million."

"I appreciate the offer of a ride, but as I've walked this far, I guess I can make it there," Monica said, as she regarded her watch.

"Addie's place is on the other side of Backhill State Forest," I said, "Literally the end of the road. It'll take you half a day to walk there from Ragged Head, which is twelve miles from here, and the hills dwarf anything you came over yesterday. I could drive you there, show you around the place, then drop you at a motel or at Enterprise. They're the only place in town to rent a car and even they close in November for the winter. Besides," I said, "if you camp out up at Addie's old place, you'll need three Ramonas to keep warm."

Monica glanced at Ramona, snoozing on the kitchen floor in a splash of sunlight, and said, "I'll take you up on the ride, but since I'm breaking my rule on imposing, I insist on buying lunch."

I agreed.

Monica helped me with the dishes, and for a few moments I was slain with grief, remembering first Ann, then Nell, drying as I washed. I could smell Ann's hair and see Nell's freckles. As Monica dried the plates and asked me to point out where they went, I realized her voice was the only one other than mine to have rung against the walls of the house since Nell's last visit.

While Monica used the bathroom, I hustled upstairs to grab my wallet and keys, Ramona fast on my heels. She sniffed around the room while I changed my pants, then bounded down the stairs ahead of me as if she'd descended them a thousand times.

When I got back to the kitchen, Monica was admiring the telescope. "Are you a stargazer?" she asked.

"Not really," I said. "Nell's an astronomer. She gave that to me when she finished her PhD. Her mother loved to stare at the night sky and knew all the brightest stars and constellations. Nell got the bug. I'm learning to use the telescope at night, but I also love scanning the fields and pond in the mornings. That's how I spied your tent."

Though I live alone, I still have a truck with a crew cab. I let Ramona jump up into the rear seat and stowed Monica's pack beside her. On the ride into Ragged Head, I explained as best I could without demonizing her, how exasperating a bully Addie had become in her old age. Monica pressed me for details, and I wanted to oblige her, but the little I knew about Addie was more rumor and gossip than firsthand knowledge. My only direct contact with her had been to examine a pond she'd wanted to expand and deepen so she could keep trout in it. Addie was abrupt, but all business.

Monica asked me to stop at the post office so she could buy stamps. She wrestled a raft of postcards and envelopes from the front pocket of her pack and ran inside while I waited in the truck with Ramona, who jumped into the front seat and whimpered a few times until Monica returned.

On the way up the mountain to Addie's farm, Monica shared the little she'd heard about Addie from her family—that Addie's parents had been exiled here because her mother's parents hadn't approved of their union, and that they'd died when Addie was young. Then she asked me to tell her anything, even if unverified, I'd heard about Addie that agreed with what she'd been told.

"The way I got it," I said, "Addie's father was a painter who took up with Addie's mother though she was much younger. She became his model and muse, and they eloped. In exchange for their promise to never contact the family again, Addie's grandparents allegedly provided the couple with a trust fund and the farm. The parents died in a car wreck. Addie inherited the property, was married briefly to a merchant sailor, then, for reasons no one could explain, retreated from society save for forays into Ragged Head for supplies or to rant and rave at town meetings."

"I'd heard Addie's mother was wild from my Aunt Carol, the only one in the family who'd talk about her."

"How are you related to Addie?" I asked.

"I think Addie's mother was a cousin of Aunt Carol's husband."

"Odd she'd be ostracized by folks she never knew," I said.

Monica shifted in her seat, "That's why I wanted to locate any friends Addie had here," she replied.

"She didn't have any," I said. "Addie liked it that way. We'd never have known she was dead if she hadn't been found by Ellie Arsenault, the mail carrier."

"Where did she find her?"

"In the house. She'd had a heart attack. We had a nasty spring storm that day, and since Addie didn't have any mail, Ellie didn't drive the last few miles out to her place. Problem was Addie had put her income tax return in her box and it had to be postmarked that evening. Addie called the postmistress and raised holy hell. Ellie drove back out and pounded on the door. When Addie didn't answer, Ellie let herself in. Found her slumped against the wall."

"Shitty way to die," Monica said.

"Unless she never knew what hit her."

"There's that," Monica replied.

We crested the hill near the entrance of the state forest. Monica turned to gaze out the window. The ridges were muted, most of the leaves wrested from the maples and oaks by a cold gale a week earlier, but the remaining color glinted like mica in the sun, and the frost slain grasses rippled in the fields as gusts swirled down from the Goodfellow Range.

"On the way back, we'll see the best view of the bay from anywhere within thirty miles," I said, "though the Goodfellow Mountains seen from Addie's place are jaw-dropping, especially in the spring when their summits are still covered in snow and the farm's fields and woods are greening up."

I walked the farm with Monica, Ramona running free, nose to the ground, divining her own history in the brown fields and shriven gardens. When she spied the pond, she rocketed in and swam across to the far side where she shook the water from her coat. Monica was quiet, eyes alert, scanning the views and pausing to drink them in. "Will this be auctioned or sold through a broker?" she asked.

"Polly Paris at Bayhead Realty is handling the sale," I said. "Addie left that up to The Humane Society. It's a rare property, but a long way from anywhere and it'd be expensive to keep up, unless one lived as frugally as Addie did. I heard Polly figures she'll advertise it in national magazines and newspapers, because it's expensive for these parts."

"I thought Ragged Head had lots of old money?" Monica said.

"It does, but they're summer folks who come for the ocean. Takes a strong person to live up here, even if it's just for the warm months, and you couldn't make a go of farming without a large family or hired help."

"You said it might go for half a million?"

"Yes."

"In Chatboro, even without a view, this property would sell for at least ten times as much," Monica said.

"If this were on the water it'd bring that much here, too," I said, "but being this far out of town on a gravel road with miles of state forest between you and your nearest neighbor keeps the price down."

We peeked into the barn and outbuildings, then peered into the house through the front porch windows. "Looks like someone still lives here," Monica said.

"Only ghosts now," I replied.

"Is the house haunted?" Monica asked with a laugh.

"Figure of speech," I said.

We admired the view, silently, from two weathered Adirondack chairs on the porch until Monica asked, "If Addie had no friends, why are there two chairs?"

"Probably so she didn't have to invite anyone inside."

Monica seemed to chew on that for a second then said, "I'd like to see inside. Do you think the broker would show me around?"

"She might," I said.

Monica pulled a cell phone from the pocket of her shorts and discovered what I could have told her—she had no service. "No bars," she said, adding without a hint of sarcasm, "that's perfect." She stowed the phone in her shorts, glanced at her watch and said, "After lunch would you mind dropping me at the realtor's office?"

"Not at all," I said, "but we'd best call Polly from town to be sure she can meet us."

We ate at Ragged Head Brewing. It was started up a while back by two local kids who have become the darlings of the chamber of commerce. Like much of Maine, Ragged Head's greatest export hasn't been lobster, but college-educated kids who've fled to Portland, Boston, and New York to find the kind of work they're qualified to do, and where they can make the kind of money that allows them to pay off their student loans and start families. Artie and Patty Stone had the good fortune to have parents who could help, but they made a choice to stay here and have done well.

When we'd been shown to a booth with a view of the water, I called Polly and set up an appointment for two o'clock, explaining that I was with someone interested in seeing Addie's farm. I could tell Polly was hesitant, but she had been a close friend of Ann's, and agreed without asking anything further.

As we were waiting for our food, Monica said, "Are you a Ragged Head native?"

"No," I said, "I was raised in Bangor, went to Colby, studied biology and worked a few years for the Healthy Coast Initiative, a nonprofit group that monitored water quality between Belfast and Lubec."

"Why did you leave that job?"

"Pay was minimal and there were so few employees that any advancement was unlikely. My mentor there, Bill Crabtree, suggested that I go to grad school for forestry. Five years later, I had my doctorate and met and married a beautiful girl from New Brunswick."

"Before I started this domestic wanderjahr," Monica said, "I was happy as a working mom and wife. When the kids were in school, I worked part-time at a large firm in Portchester. Once they'd both left for college, I threw myself into building my own practice in the hopes of retiring early and moving to the beach—Cape Cod or Rhode Island. Now that I've seen Maine, I prefer it here."

"There's an expression here that goes, 'if you can't stand the winters you don't deserve the summers.' It's easy to fall in love with us in July or when the leaves are in full color, but winter can last from late October to the tail end of April. Last May we had eight inches of snow on the ninth. And, in those months, the closer to the ocean you are, the less sun you see."

Monica smiled but didn't speak.

"Labor Day to Memorial Day, Ragged Head is just another coastal town trying to figure out a better way to live." I said. "Summer people means summer money that puts kids through college. They wait and bus tables, learn to be fry cooks, work at the marinas and country clubs, mow lawns and work long hours as landscape helpers. Some kids work retail for their parents, some fish with their fathers, but they all work every hour they can to afford an education and leave for more remunerative pastures.

Cynics say we're a town composed of Raggies—poor folks—and heads—weed smoking Trustifarians."

"In Chatboro, too, but our trust fund babies play tennis and favor expensive wine to weed."

"Some of the poorer kids here get into meth or oxy. And it's getting worse. DEA busted two labs near here last year and four women under the age of thirty committed suicide or unintentionally overdosed on oxy in a three-month span."

"That's pretty bleak," Monica said.

"It is," I said, "but if you don't have money, this is a hard place to make any. The lobster men do best, but if you're not born to it, working up from a stern man to affording your own license and boat is a daunting task. Still, some kids see that as a better bet than getting a degree and owing sixty grand when they're done."

"Is the problem lack of money or initiative?" Monica asked.

"Depends on who you ask. I'd say it's lack of confidence and experience as much as lack of capital. For generations, many kids took up the family trade. That's still true for some lawyers and business owners, but the year-round population has shrunk so much we don't have a full-time doctor and the last dentist decamped to Bangor about five years back."

"So, I wouldn't be able to build a law practice up here?"

"You might scare up enough work," I said, "but getting paid could be a bigger problem. Maine doesn't have public defenders. Instead they farm those cases out to attorneys who'll take what the state pays. I hear it's minimal. The only lawyer to come to town other than the son or daughter of one already here is Stan Sparks. He came up from Boston after his wife left him. He's been here five or six years. I only know him because he's also rustled up a few clients for me. Most of the time he's working on DWIs, domestic abuse, criminal speeding, or divorces."

"Sounds familiar," Monica said.

She was quiet as we ate, speaking only to mention how much she was enjoying her club sandwich and salad, and to ask how I liked my tomato basil soup and turkey panini.

Monica insisted on paying and did so with cash. I was surprised that she would carry so much while tramping about. I rarely have more than forty bucks with me, as I prefer to use my debit card to keep track of where my money goes.

Ramona, who'd been sleeping on the front seat, sat up and barked as we approached the truck. Monica leashed her, and we walked across the street and down the block to Polly's office, Ramona sniffing the sidewalk. At the steps to Polly's office Monica offered me the leash.

"I'm sure we can bring Ramona inside," I said, though I took the leash from Monica's outstretched hand.

"I wouldn't want to start off on the wrong foot with Polly. Do you mind?"

"No," I said.

"Besides," Monica said, "she might need to pee."

I walked Ramona up and down the block twice. Each time I passed the real estate office, I saw Monica, her back to me, talking to Polly who sat at her desk in front of the main window. It was warm for October. Clouds were building in from the water, as the horizon melded with the bays and the islands disappeared in haze. I decided to show Ramona the dog park across the street.

I closed the gate to the deserted park and let Ramona off the leash. She put her nose to the hard earth, sniffed the perimeter of the park, and after a few moments located a proper place to do her business. After a dozen circumnavigations of the little park, Ramona sighed, circled a spot in the grass, lay down, and slept. I sat on a small bench and looked out at the bay. I thought of the way I had spied the dog and Monica through the telescope and how, had I looked even ten minutes later, I would have missed them. I've been neither celibate nor promiscuous since Ann passed, but the women I've dated for any length of time were either younger than I am and wanted children or were my age and lived by inflexible rules and habits that I found suffocating. I kept an eye on Polly's office to be sure to see Monica when she came out. The longer I waited the more I wondered what was being discussed. Was Monica asking about Addie, or was she inquiring about buying the place? I couldn't imagine it was the latter, as my only experience with love at first sight was Ann.

A few minutes short of an hour after she went in, Monica and Polly stepped out of the office. Polly handed something to Monica who said, "Thanks ever so much." At the sound of Monica's voice Ramona woke and sprinted to the gate. I put her back on the leash and we crossed the street.

"I am so sorry," Monica said, "I completely lost track of time. That was rude."

"It's fine," I said, "and Ramona got to sniff the history of the dog park without any other distractions." I paused a second then said, "Was Polly helpful?"

"She was," Monica said. "She told me what she knew about Addie, including some salacious rumors regarding her husband. The place isn't officially for sale yet, which is why there's no lock box on the house. She's offered to show me around tomorrow."

"It's none of my business," I said, "but are you considering buying the place?"

"Yes," she said. "I'd need to work some things out in Chatboro, but all the time I've been walking and hiking, I have been thinking about creating a life as different from the one I've lived as is possible without going into crime. If I sell my practice—even when it's in mothballs—and my condo, I can do it. That assumes The Humane Society and I can reach a deal, but I have an idea that might intrigue them."

"I shouldn't pry," I said.

"No, it's fine, and I'd love to run my plan by you," Monica said, "though I fear I've taken up far too much of your time."

"Time, I have plenty of," I said. "Would you like to tell me over dinner at the house?"

"Polly called the woman who owns The Sea Breeze Cottages and got me a two-night reservation. She has a few heated cabins and, as a favor to Polly, said she'd take me and Ramona."

"But she doesn't serve food," I said, "and she's three miles out of town."

"I also called Enterprise and they have a car for me."

"Then we should head over there," I said.

On the way to Enterprise, Monica sketched out her plan to buy the farm from The Humane Society and allow them to use the barns and fields as a rescue facility for abused or abandoned horses and livestock—something Polly had said the board had been discussing before deciding to sell the place.

When I asked Monica if she intended to run the operation she laughed and said, "Not at all. I'd let the society find the right people for that; let them fix up some living quarters in the outbuildings, or put one up. I'd live in the main house in the good weather and find an office with a small apartment here in town. It'll be years before there's cable out there and I'd need that to work."

"Addie didn't admire many folks' ideas," I said, "but she might be fine with that."

I couldn't talk Monica into dinner. She insisted that I'd been more than generous with my time. I ached to tell that I'd had the best day in months, but was afraid that if I did I'd seem desperate in some unsavory way.

"Now that I know the way, I'll drive into town and get a few things at the supermarket. I'm going to turn in early. I'm meeting Polly at eight to go out to Addie's place, and I want to get back to Chatboro tomorrow night," she said, "but I do want to stay in touch. Let me put your numbers in my phone."

Monica punched my landline and cell numbers into her phone, then asked for my mailing address. "You've been inordinately kind to me and Ramona," she said.

"I had a great day," I replied, with greater exuberance than I'd intended. "I don't get many visitors, and I haven't been up the mountain in years."

"You were right about the view on the way back," Monica said as she pushed her phone back into her pocket, "It's a rare sight." She took my hand. Her shake was firm and her eyes sparkled. "I'm sure I'll see you again, and I would ask for a rain check on dinner."

"Anytime," I said.

Monica turned and unlocked the cottage door, called to Ramona who was lying in a pool of pale afternoon light splashed across the lawn. She hoisted her pack up from the steps, let

Ramona into the room, spun toward me and said, "Thanks, Adam."

★★★

A week later, I received a thank you note from Monica, written in perfect school teacher cursive bordering on calligraphy. All she mentioned about the farm was that she was in contact with Polly. A Christmas card said little more. Then one sleety Sunday night in April I got a call from Howard Brighton, chairman of The Humane Society board, who asked if I'd look at some plans for timber harvesting on Addie's place. My heart sank, as I was certain that Monica had decided not to buy the place and the society was looking for revenue to offset the work they felt had to be done before the property went on the market.

"When's good for you?" I asked.

"Hell, I'm retired. I'm free anytime, though the buyer is coming up in two weeks," Howard said.

"Addie's place has been sold?"

"Figured you knew," he replied, "Polly said the Mays woman was a friend of yours."

I acted as if I was less in the dark than was the case and said, "Didn't know things with Monica had been finalized."

"Took a bit, she's a lawyer you know, but we gave her a great price for allowing us to set up an equine rescue operation there. Doug Randall's son, the older one, David, is a large animal veterinarian somewhere in Vermont, but he wants to come home. He took a part-time job in Calais and he and his wife have agreed to oversee the operation. Only took so long because Monica wanted to find some grant funding for the start-up. Woman is a ball of fire. Hope she sticks."

"I do, too," I said.

I met Howard the next morning. He gave me a folder with the harvesting proposal, explaining that the trees were to be felled and sent to Tenney's Sawmill to be made into lumber for a small, timber-framed house to accommodate the rehab staff, who'd stay there on a rotating basis. Monica had sited the building on a knoll so the Goodfellow summits and a sliver of the bay would be visible in fair weather.

The night's sleet had changed to a wet snow. In town it was melting on the roads, but it was accumulating on Back Hill State Forest Road Forest, and as I steered my truck around the potholes and over the frost heaves, I thought about poor Ellie Arsenault driving out to Addie's and finding her dead in her hallway. Ann was half Addie's age when she collapsed and died from an aneurism. She taught at a community college, so many of her students were non-traditional, often middle-aged adults who'd returned to school to finish degrees begun decades before, or first-timers who'd lost their livelihoods when the mills and canneries closed. I saved over a hundred letters, notes, and emails expressing both sorrow for her passing and admiration for the difference she had made in their lives. What better testament can one receive than to be told they've inspired another? Why'd Addie have twice the time Ann got?

***

Winter refused to leave Ragged Head. The mercury never crested fifty-degrees until May 7, and the ground was too soggy to skid

out the trees for the mill until the middle of the month, just a week
before horses began to arrive.

Because there wasn't time to kiln dry the freshly milled lumber,
Clarence Tenney fronted seasoned wood cut the previous year
from the section of the state forest in tree growth rotation. Monica
was disappointed but asked only that Clarence save some boards
from her trees for benches she wanted to place by the pond.

On the afternoon of the twenty-seventh of May, the first decent
day in weeks, and my fifty-ninth birthday, I drove out to see how
things were progressing at the farm. When I arrived, Monica and
Ramona were on the porch. I got out of the truck, mounted the
steps, and plopped down in the unoccupied Adirondack chair.
Monica closed a file folder balanced in her lap, took off her reading
glasses, and said, "I've been meaning to call you."

"Then I am doubly glad I came by," I said.

"I wondered when I might redeem my rain check?"

Two nights later I made the one dinner I never screw
up, barbequed pork chops in honey mustard sauce, sautéed
mushrooms, grilled sweet potato fries, a spinach and greens salad
with the thinnings from my greenhouse, and for dessert a lemon
cheesecake—though I bought that at the new bakery that opened
up next to Ragged Head Brewing.

The next Sunday Monica made me dinner at the farm. That
night we sat in the Adirondack chairs and told each other the full
stories of our sorrows.

Though we live twenty miles across town from each other, we
began to have supper together whenever we could, sometimes
meeting at Ragged Head Brewing. In time, we stopped going
home after dessert.

The first night that Monica stayed at my place, after dinner and dessert, a slow dance without music, and after we'd made love, we took the telescope onto the deck, and she asked me to show her Ann's star.

"I can't," I said, "It's near Orion and neither he nor the star are visible this time of the year."

Monica stood on the deck, barefoot, wearing only her jeans, a blanket draped around her shoulders. For several moments we stood side by side, her hand in mine, neither of us speaking. She began to shift her weight from one foot to the other as if she were dancing, then said, "If this goes the way it feels like it's going, how will Nell feel about it?"

I moved behind her and encircled her with my arms. "She'll be pleased," I said.

"And you're sure of that?"

"Yes," I said, "Nell misses her mother but she's always telling me how I should get out and meet people. How about your boys?"

"They can't wait to come up here. They're both fly-fishermen."

"The pond and stream will please them," I said.

Monica turned and kissed me, "It's hard for me to imagine that you've been that much of a recluse," she said. "Were you?"

"Guess I was waiting to be found," I said.

"Funny," she said, "I thought you found me."

***

A Monica Mays Attorney at Law sign graces the front of the second floor above Wind and Waves Laundromat and Dry Cleaners. I helped her hook up her computer and printer the Friday of Memorial Day weekend when a small moving van and two men arrived with the furniture from her office in Chatboro. On Tuesday she had three teenaged clients from away with well-heeled parents who'd been charged with public intoxication and disorderly conduct.

***

By July, though unfinished, the rehab staff quarters were habitable, and the barns had been readied for the first horses. When the first six arrived, they were gaunt and skittish, but soon Dave Randall, his wife, and the volunteers were nursing them toward better health. By mid-August there were ten more horses of various ages and sizes on the mend, which meant that all the stalls were full. Monica has twenty acres of pasture, and two of hay, but during September trucks brought hundreds of bales the volunteers stacked in the hayloft, which had been shored up over the summer.

There were few secrets in Ragged Head, and now with social media, the gossip wire hummed at the speed of light, so when I called to tell Nell that I was seeing Monica she said, "Monica is tall, athletic, quite pretty, a lawyer from New York, and she bought Addie's old place where you are spending quite a bit of time."

I tried to speak but felt like my tongue was caught in a snarl of fishhooks.

"Dad," Nell said, "I'm stoked for you. I can get away for a weekend soon. Can I come up and meet her?"

"Of course, Nell. This is your house, too," I said.

"Great," she said, "I'll bring my friend, Phil. You'll like him."

I pressed her for details but came up empty. I figured she might bring Phil so she had someone else to appraise Monica, or maybe she was serious about him and figured there'd be no better time to tell me.

On a day in late September when brisk autumnal winds raced down from the Goodfellows, I sanded and painted the twin Adirondack chairs. I recalled telling Monica that there were two chairs so Addie wouldn't have had to invite anyone inside. I'm no longer sure of that. I wonder now if she was waiting for someone she expected who never arrived or just needed to be found.

Samuel's Hands

by Mary E. Plouffe

I n his bright yellow slicker, the man who appeared at my door looked like a giant.

"A tad more'n six-foot-three" he told me sheepishly when I asked, but his shoulders spanned my doorway, and I'd have guessed another two inches at least. A quiet shyness contrasted with his physical presence, and when I asked why he'd come, he answered simply:

"I need to figure out some stuff. Ain't nothing much harder to get at than the truth."

Samuel was not a simple man. I've lived too long in this coastal Maine community to make that mistake. He arrived in overalls, if he came straight from his boat, and left his dirt-stained rubber boots at the bottom of the stairs to my office, but that meant nothing. People here lead simple lives. They are not simple people.

He sat on the edge of the couch, leaning into our talks, hands outstretched and reaching, moving in time to his story. I was often distracted by those hands: giant upholstered creatures he never put by his side. Years of lobstering and commercial fishing had weathered them, polishing the skin to burnished leather. But it was not their texture that drew me to them, it was their size. Like the swollen muscles of a weightlifter, they loomed out of proportion to his body, dwarfing even the thick arms and shoulders that stemmed them. When he cried, he needed only one hand to cover his face: thick fingers broad enough to mask both eyes while his palm cupped his chin. He sat rolling side to side; wounded sobs escaping from behind the hand.

Sometimes he gazed at his hands, propping both elbows on his knees, and laying the palms up side-by-side ten inches from his face as though he was inspecting a fish. In those moments, the hands became a mirror, and over the months we met, I watched him find anger, sadness, and regret seeded among the calluses, embedded in the deep creases in his palms.

"My whole life, I've worked with these," he mused. "Grabbed, caught, trapped, pulled. Now it seems like everything's getting away. Seems like my final catch is going to be loss."

And so, we talked of loss.

The loss of two sons, whose talents he supported even as they took the boys far away from the island life he loved, and the fishing that fed his soul.

"They were not mine to keep," he said, "only to launch, but I hoped, so hoped, one might stay."

The loss of a curly-haired three-year-old daughter whose raging virus beat out a race over winter seas to the mainland hospital on a night he can never forget.

"I hated the ocean for a while after that," he said. "She's a cruel mistress. The tithe she took from me that night can never be repaid."

In time, the loss of his wife, who'd found island fishing life too small, too stifling, and once the children fledged, took wing herself. "I think she looked at me and saw all she'd lost; all the things I'd taken from what might have been."

And now, what brought him to my door, the loss of believing in his own choices, most frightening of all.

Always, it came back to those hands.

"I needed to work with these," he said, "I still do." And as we parsed the cost of that, and tallied what he lost, he repeated that wistful thought, "Ain't nothing much harder to get at than the truth."

One day I asked what that statement meant to him, and where it came from. He smiled, let his hands drop gently and fold into each other as he lifted his head and began:

"Oftentimes, to win us to our harm,
The instruments of darkness tell us truths:
Win us with honest trifles; to betray us
In deepest consequence."

"Shakespeare?" I asked.

"Macbeth," he answered. "It's that scene where his friend tries to warn him that the three witches can't be trusted, that they'll tell you small things that are true but lie to you about the important stuff. I guess I have my own three witches."

"Anyway," he said with a laugh, "the short version works better on the boat."

Near the end of our time together, when the loss had etched its way through rock and found fresh soil to water, he arrived one day carrying a bucket of shrimp. Hundreds of still-squirming, tiny Maine creatures captured in a metal bucket that dripped on my rug. He handled it with two fingers. I knew I would need both arms to carry it down to my kitchen after he left.

"I'll take 'em back if you can't use 'em," he offered.

I smiled.

We both knew I'd be up past midnight, until my hands ached, snapping the heads off, peeling translucent shells away from the tender pink bodies, dropping perfect thumbnail-sized gems into a bowl.

Paint It Black

by Karen Menzel

U p a gray highway like an elephant's back waves crash against a rugged coastline. No sand, but rocks like skulls. It's the road *upta camp*, and that's the only name it's ever had. You've made a nest in the back seat with the sleeping bags, and you and the dog shed black hairs all over. You've been listening to "Paint It Black" through your headphones for two hours nonstop. Dad won't pull over—he wants to beat the wicked nor'easter and get unloaded before the rain comes.

It doesn't feel like "a much-needed vacation." It feels like going into exile.

"But you love lobster rolls, honey." Dad's girlfriend rubs out her cigarette. "I'll pick you up one in town every weekend." As if a lobster roll made up for missing a summer of carnivals, drive-in movies, amusement parks, and skateboarding with friends. A summer taking the train down to Boston. A summer riding bikes in and out of small coastal towns that stretched all the way up to Canada, almost without a break in between. A summer kissing Timmy down cellar at his mom's. Timmy, who said you could ride your bike all the way down the east coast to Florida, where all the old people live.

You don't answer her, pretending you can't hear her through the headphones. She doesn't bother talking to you again.

You can't even ride a bike properly where you're going. The roads are gravel and dirt, which takes all the fun out of bikes, even though Dad's strapped your dirt bike to the trunk. An isolated cabin in the woods for family time, but there's only so many moose puzzles and cribbage a girl can take. You hug the dog, Queen of Sheba. At least you and Sheba have each other in exile.

Dad points out every lighthouse, as if they were interesting. The only interesting fact you remember is that a lighthouse keeper's cat is responsible for the extinction of a species of New Zealand bird. Single-handed? Single-pawed? Anyway, one cat. Tabby? Tibbles. Does anyone still live in lighthouses, you wonder? Are they still even used? It doesn't matter, because soon you turn into the woods and leave the green sea horizon behind.

The woods go on forever, though it feels like you're going faster, and it's so dark from the storm and sunset that Dad's turned on the headlights. Tree trunks flash past, the road ahead like a throat, the forest swallowing you. Your song plays again and again.

You helped paint silhouettes of The Rolling Stones for prom and there are still flecks of black paint on your fingernails. How long can you keep them there to remember civilization? Probably not long. Timmy's flannel still smells like him. And, if you're honest, now a little like dog, too. You'd listen to another song, but you haven't had coverage for hours and it's the only one you had downloaded. Stupid.

Dad says something you don't hear, but a tone in his voice makes you sit up and unplug one ear. "You missed a bear." He's amused. You look back down the dark road, but you only see a faint red reflection of taillights on blacktop. You slump back down and shove your headphone back in your ear. "Soak it up, kid. No electronics after we get there." Dad's cheerful voice cuts through the guitar solo.

Parents are the literal worst.

You know you've arrived because Sheba gets up and is stepping on you to look out the windows even before you notice the car's slowing down. She always knows. Even in the dark. Dad opens the back door and she leaps out to run around the car, the cabin, the car, your dad, the cabin, his girlfriend, the car. The headlights are on and the car dings nonstop while Dad and Gina unload. You have no idea why your dad calls it a camp. It's a cabin, like every cabin in every horror story. You take a moment to try and excite yourself about the prospect of *The Cabin in the Woods* or *Blair Witch* or *Evil Dead* making your summer more interesting, but then surrender. Maybe you can hide the cribbage board under your bunk bed.

Three months of no Netflix, no video games, no smartphone. Like cavemen. On the upside though, cave-teens did not have to shave their legs or go to gym class, so there's that.

Your room looks exactly like it did last summer. The Owls of North America poster is still marked with peeling stickers next to Barred, Great Horned, Screech. Someday you'll see a Hawk or Snowy. The hope of getting one of those tries to lift you.

"Kelli. Turn in time." Dad's voice is louder here at camp than at home. Probably all that particle board paneling. You clutch your phone like a lifeline and delay, but there's no point to it. When you come out into the front room, Gina's already gotten a fire going and Dad is standing at the kitchen table with the Buddha Box.

You've always called it that, because it has the backward three with a fox tail and a fez on top yoga instructor tattoo. He'd gotten the box two summers ago after you teased him about checking his phone too much on vacation. You hate yourself for that now, because it's meant two phoneless summers for you, too.

"Thirteen-year-old me was a total idiot," you say. Gina suppresses a laugh and joins you and Dad. The three of you form a small triangle around the table. With a flourish, Dad sets his phone into the wooden box.

"I see your phone," Gina says, placing her phone in the box, "and I raise you a bad habit." The red and white Marlboro box crinkles as she sets it on top of her phone.

You can't believe it. Gina has chain-smoked cigarettes since the day you met her.

"Oh ho!" Dad grins. He likes a challenge, your dad. He looks around the cabin, as if some bad habit or other is going to materialize. You consider suggesting he could put his snoring in the box and then it would be a gift to everyone, but he pulls a magnetic bottle opener off the fridge before you can open your mouth. "This symbolizes all alcohol," he grimaces as he puts the opener in the box. "If you do a no smokes summer, I'll do a dry summer. But if you cave, the deal is off."

"Same deal from my end." Gina's smile twists, a little ironic, a little self-satisfied. "You sip, I smoke." You can't imagine your dad spending a day without a Bud Light, much less a whole summer. Gina will probably have her smokes back by tomorrow.

You put your phone in the box, and both adults pause. The pressure builds. What can you give up? You're already giving up your phone, Timmy, bike riding. Everything else you would rather be doing this summer. You remember dumb, thirteen-year-old you, the one who wanted her dad to put down his phone and play with her. Then-you loved the woods, time with Dad, even enjoyed getting to know Gina, back then. Dumb-you seemed to enjoy life a whole lot more than now-you. Now-you is angry when she's not sad, tired and heavy, beaten down.

An owl hoots somewhere in the woods. It's black as coal out the window.

"Just a sec." You head outside and look around the fire pit. There. You come back inside and lower a coal-dark rock into the box, adding your phone on top. You don't want to have to explain what the rock stands for. Neither adult asks you for an explanation anyway.

"Same deal." You shut the lid and already feel lighter.

Outside, Sheba starts barking, and a squirrel runs through the door you left open, the dog hot on its heels. Gina screaming, Dad hollering. You can't help laughing, even when a lamp crashes to the ground, even when the squirrel runs into your bedroom and across your bed. Laughing, and surprised by it. You don't know how long it can last, but you'll see if you can't put that sound on repeat instead.

Seeing the Light

by Cynthia Graae

T he local radio station touted perfect conditions on the Night of the Shooting Stars, as my family called the Perseids at their peak. No moon. No clouds. On Tear Cap, far from interference of electric lights, we expected to watch meteors craze the sky for hours. The Milky Way glowed star-studded silver above us, but drops glinted in our flashlight beams. The cloudless sky was spewing rain and had been since we reached the treeless granite boulders. We were getting wet.

We were a dozen climbers, children and adults related by birth or marriage, most bonded by a fascination with comets, eclipses, sun spots, halos around the moon, dust trails, water spouts, you-name-it freak overhead occurrences, and summer-long water fights. I say *most* because my husband, Steffen, a lawyer and a man of words, would have preferred crime show reruns to a hike up Tear Cap—but there was no television where my family vacationed in Hiram, Maine. That he didn't "get" my family—engineers, computer programmers, a doctor, and that ilk's wannabees—was apparent from the beginning. The first time he came to dinner, one of my sibs, probably Carol, the good sister, land-mined his place at the table with our family's finest—a collapsing fork and a knife with a fly glued to the blade. She stuck the sieve-like spoon into the sugar bowl. When the sugar fell through the spoon, Steffen asked, "Is this any way to treat a guest?" I had to admit, in my family—yes.

They didn't "get" him, either. He made up facts, a proclivity that didn't strike them as funny or interesting. They preferred reality. Especially weird reality, like this rain. That he was married to me, the family oddball, didn't help his case. Under the circumstances, he hiked gamely.

My sister, Eugenia, who calls herself—I'm not kidding—The Great One, was leading. She's the sort to hike up Mount Katahdin at 3 a.m. to see the green flash over the Atlantic in that split second before dawn.

But maybe her prowess was waning—she was leading us straight into rain.

My brother, Walter, supervised the sewers of a New Hampshire city; Carol was married to a doctor who had studied geology in college; Eugenia, as she herself will tell you, knew absolutely everything. With these credentials, they fancied themselves as water experts. As we continued our flashlight climb over sloping boulders, they postulated causes for the cloudless rain. Droppings from night-flying birds? Melting ice from meteors? Water bugs? Waterspouts from mountain springs? When Walter suggested spray from the Atlantic, twenty-five miles away, Eugenia, ever needing to be right, announced, "This rain makes no sense."

"Oh, it does," Steffen said. "I'll explain." The path ahead went dark as flashlight beams swept accusingly in his direction. He's a Democrat and he's married to that one (me), they were thinking, so how could he possibly know a thing?

Steffen spoke with confidence about how the earth cools at night causing moisture to evaporate, and how the air becomes supersaturated and then re-forms as mist that dissipates so quickly it seems to be invisible. The way he joined concepts together was—well—I could practically hear *Ah has* and *Oh wows* exploding through my family's dedicated-to-science brains. Even Eugenia, programmed to lob missiles at all ideas except her own, was impressed.

A family discussion followed. My three sibs, with a little help from the kids, as we called the next generation, concluded we'd be able to see the shooting stars through the rain. Flashlight beams arced back to the path, and we resumed our upward trek.

Soon Walter called out, "Hey, Steffen, if you're so right, why haven't we seen this kind of rain before?"

That really got me. I almost shouted, "You can explain volcanoes, can't you, but have you ever seen one?" But Steffen jumped in to explain that the unusual conditions that night—the really clear sky, absence of a moon, temperature, ionization, and relative humidity—were right for this rare phenomenon.

His voice was drowned by gasps. A panorama of skyscrapers lit up the far horizon.

But we were in Maine, east of the White Mountains and west of Portland. No cities, towns, or rural villages had been visible from Tear Cap before, and it was not possible that we were witnessing a spurt of urban growth.

Except that towers were there.

My sibs hypothesized. Could those shining towers be the last rays of the sunset two hours before? In our confusion about the rain, had we turned toward Portland? Carol asked Steffen if the night's strange atmospheric conditions could be throwing a once-in-a-lifetime reflection of Boston or New York high into the sky.

"Beats me," he said.

At that exact moment, Eugenia shouted in her best eureka voice, "The Northern Lights."

Instant recognition flashed through the group. The Great Eugenia was right. Those who know my childhood family would understand the dream-come-true of those flares from thousands of miles away. A first for us all. Even the kids who had no idea of Northern Lights were stunned silent.

We stared as the towers shimmered, dipped, and rose again, and long after they faded to dark.

On the way down, the kids discovered that Walter had been dousing us with his super soaker—another episode in a summer-long water fight. Eugenia announced, "Revenge." Carol said, "I bought more water balloons and materials for building a catapult." The kids cheered.

Before we reached the junipers, Steffen stopped. I was surprised that the entire group gathered around him.

He stared into the distance where the blazing flares had been, as if the dark horizon itself was another nocturnal phenomenon. The rest of us stared, too.

We sank into the silence of knowing we might never see the aurora borealis again.

Rain at Hurd's Pond

by Michelle Soucy

First you hear, but don't feel:
From the highest leaves and canopy of hemlocks,
a gentle tapping, like the sound of falling in love.
The air becomes wool-colored
and "Oh, it's raining!" someone will say.
And you will look out toward the water
and see the silent silver rings popping here, there, here-there,
and the creamy lilies' pads slowly shivering in the soft rise and fall of almost-waves
"Oh yeah," you will say. "It's raining."
"Funny how we don't feel it in here under the trees," someone else will move to coax
the smoldering campfire. "Funny how we're protected here."

"Yes," you will say. Yes. You will think of the laughter that drifted from within tents
in long deep black nights of cold Maine summers you'd wished never would end,
laughter and voices of people no longer living—both friends and family—
and now their laughter springs up in the raindrops, their love
glimmers within the layers of tree rings, touches you when you brush past the caress
of cedar leaves; their breath is the brisk air you're breathing.

You will remember the golden contentment of campfire reflection in their eyes when
they were here,
when you were all here
together
    sitting on the armchair-sized chunks of granite
    drawing in the scent of warm copper-colored pine needles that coat the earth,
    stirring the cracking, sparking firepit with a burnt-tipped stick,
    sipping from a cup of tart, powder-mixed lemonade or, later, a cool wet beer bottle,
telling stories—both made-up and true—and exaggerated memories,
talking about the way things are or should be or could be or never will be in the world.
The chipmunks and red squirrels all the while would trill and scatter,
the bullfrogs groaned like foghorns, taking stock of the day,
the owls would tell you: *Me too, I'm here, too, behind you in the trees, me too,*
and the loon on the far dark and sequestered end of the pond would call
like a lonely mother summoning her children, *It's good here, good. It's good to come home.*

Then you will feel a pin-speck of rain on the top of your cheek
and another on your lower lip
and someone will say, "Time to go into the tent, maybe."
You will tilt your head all the way back
and peer into the white shimmering piece of sky that the treetops kindly let show,
and the raindrops will tick the metal tent poles like something hot beginning to cool,
and you will say, "I think I'll stay outside a bit longer."
Because, really, and always, you are protected here.

A Stranger

by Clif Travers

October, 1956

I ain't much for the Bible, but even I know the story of the apple. It's all about sin and temptation and how a snake talked Eve into eating one after God told her not to. It's a good story, but I don't need no fiction. I got my own story of the apple, and it's a shameful one. It's strange how one little thing can change a person. I used to eat an apple every day, just like that rhyme tells ya. But I haven't in nearly thirty years. Now, all I gotta do is see one and I nearly break down crying, thinking of that poor man, that day, and how bad a person I was. So I won't touch the things, 'cept the one I place at his stone every year. Always the same kind. Always on the twelfth of October. Least I can do.

I can't forget the day, even though I've drunk enough to wash it away ten-times over. All these years and it's still there, wedged in with the good and the bad, which there's lots more of than I'd like. It's far clearer than the others. I wonder why that is, why the one memory you wish you could dig out and burn manages to stay put longer than any of the ones you'd like to hold tight to the

end. I suppose it's 'cause of the guilt I've harnessed to it. It's there
to remind me that I am not a good woman, not then or now.

October 12, 1956. Gorgeous day. Fall colors against deep blue.
Indian summer in Maine, that final gift of the kinder season before
the hellish one is heaped upon us. There was a hefty breeze,
real warm and summery, coming up off the river, and we mill
girls—the four of us—were making a ridiculous show of trying to
control our skirts against it. Jane joked that we were like Marilyn
Monroes, and we truly thought we were, all giggly as if the
wind was being naughty and we were mildly offended by it.
Course we weren't, strutting our young legs down Depot Street,
clutching our groceries with one hand and barely keeping our
undies covered with the other. It was always us four: Jane, plain as
her name, with straight dark hair and lips so thin and hard they
could split wood; Wilma, who mighta been a beauty if only her
ma had cared enough to teach her something like how to style
her hair instead of wearing it in a knot so tight it made her eyes
slant; and Fattie Lattie—as we used to call her—always grumpy,
couldn't muster a smile to save her life. She was my Johnny's
sister. A Thompson, so naturally snooty. Never liked me much.
Always looked at me sideways like she didn't trust me fully and
was waiting for me to show my true colors. Lattie was smarter
than she looked.

We'd just done our shopping at Johnson's after a full day at the
mill, so the clean warmth was nice against our bare legs. It swirled
up and tickled at the dark and sweaty parts. In those days, the
mill whistle blew at 3:30, and the women were let out a half-hour
before the men so we'd be all cleaned up and ready with dinner
and such. It was all about the men and what they'd need after a

long day—as if ours weren't longer. So we were walking fast and talking over each other like we always did on Fridays, laughing about another stupid girl who'd found herself up a stump without a husband. We weren't being mean or nothing, just doing what we do in small towns to pass the time, gloating at our own good fortune at getting hitched before the babies got in us.

We were halfway down Depot Street, nearly to Main, when we heard the horn blast and the sound of brakes. If I live to a hundred, I won't forget the sudden loudness of it. Shot right through the afternoon, it did. You don't hear sounds like that here. Not in Riverton. Quiet place. Even horns don't get worked 'cept to scare a cow or a deer outta the way. Everybody within a mile musta known something bad had happened.

"Jesus, Mary, and Joseph," one of us yelled. And being the kinda girls we were—the kind to not miss nothing that might change the pace—we were off and running. We had to hug our bags tight so we wouldn't lose anything. Jane was in the lead with her big thighs that came from riding. Wilma and Lattie were next, so close to each other I thought Lattie's swaying hips would send Wilma flying. I lagged behind, cursing the weight of a pork roast I'd bought for Johnny. I was in my early days of wifing then, still trying to please a husband through his belly. Fool's errand.

When I finally got to the corner, I couldn't see much. Must have been twenty mill girls in front of me. I had to stand on tiptoes to peer over shoulders and around heads. But I was pretty skinny back then, compared to most Riverton women, and I was able to squeeze between Natalie from the spool shop and her fleshy daughter, Grace. I pushed my way to the curb, and from that point, so close I could see everything, it was like a scene out of a newspaper. That's how I remember that part: real detailed, and kinda black and white and still. Folks had come outta the restaurant, the post office, and even the Hogpenny where "lazy, useless men drink away their lives," as Grammie used to say. All eyes on both sides, even the drunken ones, were on the center of the road, a few feet in front of Mr. Johnson's van.

That's where the man was, splayed across the asphalt like something that fell outta the sky, one arm stretched toward a bag of groceries. Traffic, much as we get in Riverton, was stopped in both directions, and everything was quiet as if the volume of the day had been turned way down. Even the wind had quit, like it was holding its breath, like we all were.

Then, in the middle of all that stillness, something moved. It was just an apple, but we all turned to it 'cause it was the only thing moving. It tumbled out of the man's fallen grocery bag, rolled and rolled real slow, and finally stopped, just like that, inches from the man's face. Strangest thing I'd ever seen. It was like it had purpose or something, like someone was calling it or pulling it with an invisible string.

From where I was standing, no more than a couple feet away, I could see that the man watched it, too. His eye, the one that wasn't pressed into the road, followed it as it rolled to him. And when it stopped in front of his face he looked right at it. Stared *into* it, it seemed. That's when I noticed the kind of apple it was. It was the very same as the ones I'd just bought, the expensive kind I'd planned on baking with brown sugar and a little whiskey. Something special for Johnny.

I'd seen the recipe in *Coronet Magazine*. It was supposedly one of Grace Kelly's, and everybody knows she's got good taste. It called for these expensive varieties that I'd never heard of. Johnson's had them, which surprised me, but I had to ask for them 'cause they kept them in a special place in the back, probably so folks wouldn't steal them. They'd cost me twenty cents a pound. I remember 'cause it was a lot to spend on apples in those days. I'd looked them all over, smelled them, felt for bruises. I suppose I was trying to decide if Johnny and me were worth such pricey fruit. The girls were rushing me, telling me to "just buy the damn things." So I finally did—bought four so we'd have 'em for Sunday, too. Turns out they never made it that far.

It occurred to me, as I stared at the expensive apple just lying there in the dirt of the road, that the man might have bought it for his supper, too, maybe even a special supper for somebody. Or maybe it was something to snack on during a long drive home. I could tell he wasn't from around here. His suit and shoes were nice, like something not out of a catalog. And there was a hat that must have fallen off when the van hit him; it was one of those straw ones and it had a pretty feather in it. Not something a Riverton man would dare to wear. Nope, the man was a stranger in town. It was clear.

I felt bad for Mr. Johnson. He'd been sitting in his van this whole time, probably in shock, not knowing what to do, maybe even praying. I could see his lips moving, and then he finally got out, came around to the front, and just stood over the man, pleading with him to get up, asking if he was all right, which he obviously was not. I think Mr. Johnson was crying a little. He looked around at us, his face all red and squished up. We were all being stupid, just standing there, staring like we were watching a play or something.

"What should I do? Tell me what to do." He'd always seemed like a weak man, but now he looked damn pathetic.

I felt bad for him but I didn't know what to do neither. Never seen somebody hit by a car before.

"I'll ring up the sheriff." It was Mrs. Abbott from the hotel. "Better not touch him."

Folks were leaning in, and I could feel Grace's big, sweaty boobs on my back, but I couldn't move. I was already closer than I cared to be. And it was 'cause of that closeness that I saw things nobody else could've, not the way his head was, all twisted to the side. I could clearly see his eye, and it was staring at the apple, right *into* it, it seemed. And then—and I swear it—the man grinned. Lying there, belly down and all bent around, he smiled at the apple. It wasn't a big smile, but it was there.

Now, I'm not a thinking person. Never was. In fact, I prefer not to do much of that, 'specially if it's none of my damn business. But that day, that moment, I was thinking a lot. It was 'cause I was so close to him, closer than anybody else. I think that's why I had such a sense of what was going through his mind. His thoughts were all about apples. I could see it. He was remembering all the apples he'd ever had, some held to his mouth by somebody he loved, some picked with his ma and pa when he was a kid. He remembered a perfect one he'd given to a teacher once, a young and pretty thing he had a crush on when he was just a boy and hadn't learned yet that apples won't buy love or better grades. But he thought, and I thought with him, about how the whole world can fit inside an apple, all the sweet and sour of this life. All the bright spots and darkness can be found right there in one juicy bite. I could see it in his eye, the one I could not look away from no matter how much I wanted. I could see it all, his ma and pa and the teacher and somebody he loved enough to share a piece of fruit with. I could even see the inside of the apple, that whole world of sweet and sour life. And it's 'cause of what I saw in his eye that I have so much guilt. I sorta knew him for a minute, saw into his soul. And then I did him wrong. In the next minute, the eye lost focus like it was pulled away from the apple and from all the world. It got dark, the smile went away, and there was no doubt he was gone.

Finally, somebody came. Too late, of course. Mr. Corson, who used his van as an ambulance whenever we needed one, drove up with his horn blasting. His son was with him, and they gently loaded the man in. Then Sheriff Wilson was there telling us to stay back while he directed the van away, down Route 27 toward the hospital in Farmington. After it left, he held traffic back so folks could cross Main Street and be on their way. The whole event, from horn blast to the man's death, couldn't have been more than twenty minutes, but it seemed longer. It made me tired all of a sudden, all that thinking about the man and what I know I saw in his eye. Made my head hurt, too. I couldn't get myself to move yet. I waved the girls on, and I sat down on the curb right near where the man had let out his final breath.

Not sure how long I was there, staring at the spot where he'd been, thinking about what I'd seen in his eye, or what I thought I'd seen. I was too shaky to stand, too full of his thoughts to have any of my own. I felt empty, but full at the same time, if that makes any sense. I didn't like the feeling, and I didn't wanna move till I felt steady and back to myself. So I just sat there on that dirty curb, all alone with that poor man's memories flooding my brain.

I didn't snap out of it till the second mill whistle blew, the one that tells the men to go home. It'd just be a few minutes before all them, including my Johnny, would be hustling down Depot Street, making a beeline for the Hogpenny, getting their beer and shot of whiskey before heading home to their women.

I stood, still feeling a little shaky, grabbed up my groceries and slapped the dirt off my rear. The apple was still in the road. It didn't look bruised or nothing, and I thought for a split second to pick it up, being such a pricey thing. I decided against that. It was in the road, after all. But truth be told, I didn't wanna touch it after what I'd seen. It gave me the willies. So I gripped my bags real close to stop the shivers, and I started walking home.

That's when I saw the wallet, just a couple feet from the curb, partly hidden by the brim of the fancy hat. It was a deep red, nearly a match to the apple. I didn't quite know what it was at first—so shiny and big, nothing like any wallet I'd seen before. More of a billfold, I guess you'd call it. I looked around, but the street was empty. The women were long gone at that point, and I could hear the men from way up on Depot, talking loud and coming my way. I didn't pause. The apple was one thing, but a wallet was something different. I balanced my groceries in one arm, snatched it up, and dropped it into a bag.

It's nearly a mile from town to what was then our new home. I had lots of time during that walk to consider the man, the apple, and the billfold. When I was far enough away from houses, where there used to be a long stretch of nothing, I stopped, set down the bags, and pulled out the shiny leather wallet. It was still warm from the asphalt, maybe even from the man. His license was in it with his name, his address, and his birth date. It's been so long now

I've forgotten all that. It was the money that caught my eye and fouled up my already rattled brain. There were six twenties, five tens, and a bunch of singles. I remember that well 'cause it was a lot of money then. Still is, I suppose.

So I took the bills, folded them and shoved them deep into the pocket of my work skirt. Then I threw the wallet as hard as I could into the woods. I'd be lying if I said it felt good to do that, to get rid of the thing and to feel the bulge of all that money in my pocket. As soon as it left my fingers I felt guilt and regret, the kind I knew would stick with me for a long time. And it surely has. There hasn't been a day since that I haven't wished I'd done what I knew damn well I shoulda. I ain't no Eve in a garden. I ain't that innocent. Even in my youth I knew what temptation does, how it can make a person lose sight. But in that moment, I didn't care about good and bad, right or wrong. All I cared about was how hard me and Johnny worked in that smelly mill, and how a few extra dollars might make us feel a little closer to happy.

I started back down the road, but at some point I musta started crying, 'cause in a few yards I could hardly see through it. I had to put the damn bags down again and swipe the wet outta my eyes. I knew Johnny wouldn't be far behind me and he'd be wondering why I wasn't in the kitchen already, doing the thing I was supposed to be doing. But when I bent to hoist up the bags again I could hardly lift 'em. One had gotten real heavy. It was the bag with the apples, of course.

I dug through it till I found all four. I cradled them in one arm and just looked at them for a minute. Somehow, they'd gotten even more beautiful than when I'd bought them. It musta been the afternoon light, 'cause they seemed to be lit from inside, like those windows in fancy churches. They truly did glow, and for a split second I just wanted to hold them like that forever, to cradle them like they were something alive, something chock-full of all sorts of possibilities.

But in the next second I got a hold of myself and did the only thing that made sense. I pulled my throwing arm back and heaved each one of them, with even more strength than I'd given the wallet, into the same woods. Hurt my shoulder a little but I kept throwing. They went high, all bright red and shiny in the afternoon, and then they got swallowed up by the dark. Each apple went a little deeper, as if my resolve got stronger. I stood there after, thinking about my actions, trying to understand them. But I eventually gave up on the thinking and hustled home.

For years after, every spring before the underbrush got thick, I went back to that stretch of woodland. I spent hours combing through the brush and layers of packed dead leaves hoping to find the billfold. It was this guilt that kept me going back. You see, the town had found no identification on that poor man and no one had come to claim him, so they'd buried him in Riverside Cemetery with a simple marker. "A Stranger" they'd called him, which was mostly the truth. I did try to remedy that, but eventually new homes were built in that stretch of woods and I had to give up.

Of course the money came in handy, but it didn't last long. Never does. I bought a few things for the house. Nothing Johnny asked about or even noticed. None of it made me feel any better, but I didn't feel so bad I needed to tell anybody. I guess that's how you know you're a truly bad person, the fact you can live with it.

But I do place an apple on the man's gravestone every October twelfth. That's something, anyway. And it is always the most perfect, the most beautiful, and the most expensive one I can find. It's the least I can do.

Fogged In

by Charlotte Crowder

R osalie was born on the island. Grew up over the ridge, on what they still today call "the dark side"—it was the last place to get electricity. She was always pretty. Those green eyes, you know, against her black hair. Married an island boy, Ben Weed. Together they moved to his family homestead in the section known as Weedville, peopled by Ben's cousins, first, second, once-removed. She had three kids in three years, the way they do hereabouts. Was widowed early. Ben's lobster boat was found circling empty off George's Bank. No sign of Ben or his sternman, my nephew, Isiah. Rosalie raised three fine children with the support of Ben's various cousins, her own family members scattered across the island, and the other townsfolk, who may as well have been family. She made a meager living working at the library the two days a week it was open, and helping me out at the general store on the opposite days.

Her kids went to high school off-island, boarding with families of fellow students. They're gone now, scattered on the mainland. Our youngsters don't stay on the island. There's nothing much here for them.

Rosalie lives over there, in the classic Cape, atop the rise, flanked by that small orchard. Has a grand view of the harbor and the fishing fleet. Weedville's a misnomer. Rosalie doesn't tolerate weeds. You can see, the house is surrounded by a riot of flowers. She tends them all spring and summer: lupines, climbing roses, hydrangeas, sweet peas, phlox, sunflowers. Her dooryard doesn't look like some. There are no old appliances stacked up in front of the house. The only rusted thing she owned, the Chevy truck Ben had ferried over from the mainland when they first married, was stowed behind the toolshed, out of sight. She's always kept the homestead immaculate. Polishes those king pine boards with bee's wax, down on her hands and knees, 'til you can see your reflection. And her larder, down cellar, the shelves are lined with the preserves she's put up. Swear she polishes the jars, too.

Ferdie used to help her out with any heavy work or whenever roof work was needed. 'Course he's too old for roof work these days.

When her mother took sick, Rosalie brought her over from the dark side. Nursed her several years. Her mother's buried over in Mount Rest Cemetery now. The whole town turned out for her funeral.

After her mother died, well, that left Rosalie pretty lonely. She found plenty to busy herself. She started making quilts for the annual raffle. Beautiful quilts they are. Every year, I cross my fingers when I buy my ticket, but I haven't been lucky enough to win one yet. That woman has golden hands.

Yes, she kept plenty busy, but was lonely. She continued at the library and I gave her a few extra hours at the general store. Not so much because she needed the money, but just to give her company.

Then five or so years ago, he came along. Far from young, but Rosalie wasn't either anymore. Still pretty she was though, if a bit plump by then. Though her hair was no longer raven black, those green eyes of hers shone. And he had a sparkle in his to match the minute he laid eyes on Rosalie. A handsome fellow, tall, good posture, big handlebar mustache, the look of a sea captain. Had a little Fox Terrier with him. His sailboat, the *Lady Jane*, was on one of our guest moorings. A gem of a small wooden sloop, varnished to a shine. He came into the general store to pay his mooring fee and looking for block ice for the boat's icebox. We were out of ice at the time. The mailboat with the delivery wasn't due for a couple of hours.

Well, didn't he just take a seat in the rocker over by the puzzle table—I keep a jigsaw puzzle, one of those thousand-piece ones, on a card table in the corner. Gives folks something to do when they come in from fishing. Depending on the puzzle, sometimes even the summer folk get interested.

He wasn't looking at the puzzle though. He was looking at Rosalie. And did he talk. He talked until the mailboat arrived and we learned just about everything there was to know about him. His name was Ralph. He went to Maine Maritime Academy years ago. But he wasn't from Maine, was from New Jersey. I'd already figured that out from his accent. He had captained an oil tanker for twenty-five years. Just retired. Had been cruising Penobscot Bay all that summer with the little dog. The dog sat upright next to the rocker, quiet as can be. He watched closely as Ralph talked and turned his head toward Rosalie and me, as if to be sure we were listening. And Rosalie was. She was rapt. I busied myself dusting the grocery shelves while I listened in.

He told us he had never married. Being out to sea for long stretches wasn't conducive to long-term relationships, he said. Well, that gave me pause.

When the mailboat finally came in, Bobby arrived at the store with armloads of packages—mostly for the summer folk. Ralph went down to the dock with Bobby and helped bring in the groceries I'd ordered for the store, along with the ice, block and cube. Helpful, I thought. A good sign.

Ralph left with three blocks of ice in a canvas bag.

Then came the fog that would hold Ralph captive on the island. For four days, the foghorn bleated like a sick sheep. We woke to fog as thick as I have ever seen. It cloaked the island in soft gray eiderdown; hid the harbor and the fishing fleet, the spiked spruce that ridged the hills; erased the buildings across the road, the road itself, and the curbstone. Sounds played the tricks they do in fog. Though most were muffled, disembodied conversations bounced off the thickened air and carried word-for-word across town. The ferry horn from over to Bass Harbor sounded like it was coming straight at the invisible town dock.

The fog draped over people as they pushed through it, so that when they appeared at the doorway, as if out of nowhere, customers were outlined in sparkling droplets. The fishermen arrived first, as they do every morning. They settled down at the puzzle table for the day. Ralph soon joined them. He was quieter that day. Sat and listened mostly, and collected a pile of all the green pieces. The summer folk showed up later. They were excited by the novelty of the fog. A few leaned over and studied the puzzle. Those who fit a piece, exclaimed loudly. But, they didn't stay.

The air in the store hung heavy with smells from the kitchen out back, first with blueberry muffins, later, toward lunchtime, with fish chowder. When I ran out of seating around the table, it was like a game of musical chairs. One of the fishermen would up and leave for a while to give another a chance at the puzzle. Ralph stayed put and the Fox Terrier sat upright beside him that whole day. Ralph leaned over and scratched him behind the ears from time to time.

Every hour or so, Rosalie would circle the table with a new pot of coffee and top off folks' cups. She and Ralph exchanged smiles. His eyes crinkled around the edges and those mustaches waggled. Rosalie wore a pretty white blouse, starched and ironed. When she reached to pour the coffee, I noticed it stretched tight across her bosom. I could see Ralph noticed, too.

Ralph put together most of the green hills and fields. The puzzle, scattered with muffin crumbs, was finished before closing time, but Ralph hung around and made small talk with Rosalie.

On the second day I took out another puzzle. Ralph was in early. He and Rosalie set out the pieces, turning each one to the proper side. The little dog was resigned to spending the day at the store. Crawled under the puzzle table, stretched out to his whole length and slept, snoring once in a while. Ralph had loosened up a bit with the fishermen by then. They shared stories of the sea.

Middle of the day, Ferdie emerged from the fog like an apparition on the front step of the store, a halo of water droplets framing his wild gray hair and scraggly beard. He brought a flyer announcing the next evening's square dance at the grange hall and tacked it up on the bulletin board.

I was busy in the back storeroom, so didn't hear Ralph's invitation to Rosalie. All I knew was that she bought a few yards of red-checked gingham before she left the store that evening. I figured she must be starting on a new quilt.

The third day was a library day, so Rosalie was not at the store. Ralph stayed all day, worked on blue patches of sky and bantered with the fishermen. Looked a bit woebegone, but he didn't seem to dare to ask after Rosalie's whereabouts.

Well now I think Rosalie must have taken that day off from the library and spent it at her sewing machine, because that evening she showed up at the grange hall in a gingham shirtwaist with Mr. Ralph beside her, his arm looped through the crook of her elbow in a proprietary way. Since way back when, I've run the food concession on dance nights. Rosalie had not been to a grange hall dance in decades. And I can't remember that she ever danced, even in her early married days. But dance she did. Watching Ralph swing her around, I remember thinking he may not have had any long-term relationships, but he sure must have had a number of short-term ones. And I still did wonder about the Lady Jane he must have named his boat after.

At the end of the dance, everyone was swallowed up in the thick gray cloud as soon as they walked out the door. So, no one in town knew whether the two went their separate ways when they left the grange. Invisible cars pulled out of the parking lot, headlights bouncing in eerie circles. The mournful tones of the foghorn sounded in the background.

On the morning of the fourth day, the island was still wrapped in a cloak of fog. Both showed up at the store, each in a clean set of clothes—Rosalie in time to open the store, Ralph an hour or so later. His little dog knew more than all the rest of us, judging by the way he trotted up to Rosalie, tail a-wagging.

By that time, the summer folk were no longer intrigued by the fog. At a loss as to what to do with their bored kids, they brought them to the store and parked them at the puzzle table, which drove Ralph and the fishermen away. Ralph stood by the cash register and watched Rosalie stock the shelves until around noon, when the fog began to lift. The outline of the buildings across the road came into view. Then a wind came up and blew the fog away. It was like tattered cloth across the sky, with the sun shining through the rents. Ralph bought ice and some provisions for the *Lady Jane*. He exchanged a few smiles and whispers with Rosalie, then headed down to the dock.

After closing, I watched Rosalie walk to the end of the dock and wave as Ralph hoisted his sails and sailed off the mooring. Well, I thought that was the end of that.

After Ralph left the island, Rosalie was moody and clumsy, dropping everything. She dropped the quart pickle jar we kept at the cash register for spare pennies. There were shards of glass everywhere and the pennies rolled down the slope of the old floorboards. For years, my grandchildren have amused themselves prying those pennies out of the crack in front of the threshold where they collected.

Then the letters started arriving. Rosalie usually only got mail from her kids. As I sorted the mail, I noted these letters were different: business-sized envelopes, addressed in penmanship with strong, right-leaning strokes. No return address, but I surmised they were from Ralph, because there were so many of them—two or three a week—and because Rosalie seemed so happy when they came. She'd disappear into the storeroom, where she ripped them open. Back behind the counter, she'd hum the rest of the day.

But my worries still weren't allayed when the postcard arrived a month or so later. Postmarked Boston, Massachusetts with a picture of the waterfront. In that same penmanship it said, "Sold the *Lady Jane*, because I know you are afraid of the water (strange for an island girl). Arriving on the mail boat, September 15th." Well, at least Lady Jane was out of the picture. But I was still suspicious. So, I mobilized the townsfolk. On a library day, when Rosalie was out of the store, I told everyone that came in about Ralph's arrival date. That was all it took; word spread like wildfire across the island.

Half hour before the mailboat was due to arrive on September 15, I filled a bucket to wash the salt spray from the store windows and carried the stepladder out in front of the store. Standing atop the ladder, I had a good view of the wharf. Several of the fishermen returned early, their boats already tied up to the town dock. Ferdie was there, helping them unload the day's catch. The harbor master strutted up and down the pier. Several folks wandered along the shore's edge. As the mailboat approached, Mrs. Dow across the way pushed her window curtain aside and peeked out.

Ralph stood on the deck, holding his little dog in his arms. As soon as the boat bumped up against the dock, the dog jumped out of his arms and ran straight to Rosalie.

Without saying a word to anyone she passed, Rosalie took Ralph's hand and walked him up to the Cape atop the hill. Ferdie headed home.

For the next few weeks, there were a few raised eyebrows, I can tell you. We needn't have worried—they were married by

Columbus Day. Up to the Baptist church on a sparkling day, with the sugar maples in full red glory against a cloudless sky.

Ralph had a new model Chevy brought in on a barge and Rosalie gave Ferdie the old, rusted pick-up.

Though he will always be from away, Ralph fits in real well here, despite that Jersey accent. He and Rosalie are happy as clams in mud. Ferdie drives that old truck down to the town dock every day. He helps Bobby unload the mailboat and drives the mail and supplies up to the store. Truck only goes in reverse these days, so he backs down to the dock, turns around, and backs up the hill to make the deliveries.

Glass

by Lara Tupper

W hen Sam turned eight, she told her father she wanted to be a *Solid Gold* dancer. They were in his shop, and he said, "Sounds good, Sammy," and she loved him for this, for not laughing. They lived in Maine, which, her father reminded her, was "about as goddamned far from *Solid Gold* as you're likely to get." He smiled when he said this, one side of his mouth moving up like a hook. He had a fuzzy, reddish beard and eyes that drooped in a friendly way.

Sam's father was a stained glass artisan, which meant he made lamps and mirrors with fancy frames and sometimes entire stained glass windows for summer people on Ocean Point. The local craft shops sold his pieces, and he had a catalog business, too, nationwide. Every November he hired an assistant to help him get through the Christmas orders.

Sam helped, too. After dinner, in front of the TV, she unraveled thin strips of copper foil from a cardboard spool, narrow strips like hair, and pressed them around glass pieces her father had cut that day. The copper foil had to be wrapped tightly around the edges, and then he soldered the shapes together. The pieces looked perfect when they were first cut. Sam was sometimes tempted to swallow them whole.

On weekends, Sam's father took her to Ocean Point to collect mussel shells, the outsides mottled blue and the insides pearly gray and smooth against her thumb. At home she dried them in the sun on the back porch until they were bleached a dull, disappointing shade, then she wrapped these with copper too. He soldered them to things for decoration—candleholders, jewelry boxes. "Made in Maine," said the labels. The shell-pieces were his bestsellers.

There were cardboard boxes everywhere in the house, filled with shells and glass and spools of copper foil. There were patterns sketched in pencil on loose-leaf paper. Dad's steel-toed boots stood by the fire like small statues. He wore thick flannel shirts. He didn't own a tie. He didn't like to dress up.

Sam's mother liked to dress up. She liked parties—New Year's, Fourth of July. For Halloween she wore old dance leotards and became a black cat or a sexy witch. She wore a kind of costume for her job, too—a matching navy blue skirt and jacket with a little red scarf around her neck. The gold name badge on her lapel was pinned exactly parallel to her left breast pocket. She was a teller at the First Federal Bank of Damariscotta, and by the time she woke Sam up for school each morning, she was already dressed and wearing pale, pink lipstick.

Lately, after work, Sam's mother liked to wear loose clothes—sweatshirts and shapeless, drawstring pants. She sat in the armchair and wrapped her hands around mugs of herbal tea. She read a lot and blew at the steam, her lips pursed in a funny o.

Sam's father, after work, sat in his chair and rolled cigarettes, slowly sprinkling tobacco into little white squares and squeezing the paper between his thumb and finger. He lit the rolled tips with a candle flame and inhaled. He nodded as Sam showed him each copper-trimmed piece.

"You don't have to," Sam's mother said, blowing. She meant the glass.

"No one's forcing her," Dad said.

Sam spread out her fingers for her mother to see. She was very careful—she almost never got cuts.

But her mother wasn't looking. "What does Hart say about the state of your hands?" Mr. Hart was Sam's piano teacher.

"Mr. Hart prefers the Carpenters to the Bee Gees," Sam said, to change the subject.

Her father sniffed. Her mother said nothing, and took her first sip of the evening. When the tea was gone, she would allow herself a different kind of drink.

***

Sam's parents used to dance together. Her mother wore tight jeans and a shirt with a wide collar and her father's beard was thicker. They took disco classes at the YMCA and practiced in the living room to the *Stayin' Alive* soundtrack, tripping on the throw rug by the fire and passing a cigarette back and forth.

"You're a natural," her father had said, kissing her mother on the lips.

Sam's mother had almost been in *A Chorus Line*. She'd auditioned before Sam was born, the summer she lived in New York City alone. Two callbacks, but not a third. Sam didn't have to ask what a callback was.

They played slow songs too. "So Far Away" and "Both Sides Now." Her father held her mother very close, hardly moving at all, and she smiled in a distracted way, her head resting on his flannel shoulder.

When they stopped taking lessons, Sam thought it had something to do with the Death to Disco sticker she'd seen in town, on a Saab with New York plates. When she was alone in the house, Sam sometimes pulled the records from their sleeves one by one, to look for nicks.

Her mother danced on her own sometimes, when her father was out. There was no music. She scooted around the living room with a Bloody Mary, with coiled urgency. It seemed private.

Sam wanted to move like that, with ease or with purpose. She wanted her mother to teach her how.

***

In ballet class, Sam wasn't allowed to wear her Bee Gees t-shirt. She had to wear pink tights and a black leotard, just like everyone else. She liked the scratchy old piano records. She liked to watch the other feet and pretend they weren't connected to other girls. Just feet. She tried to explain but Ms. Dardonne, the ballet teacher, said, "Chin up. No cheating."

Near the end of class, Ms. Dardonne pushed the bar to the side of the room. It made a terrible screeching sound, like wheels braking. The other girls lined up in groups of three, no talking allowed. Sam followed.

Ms. Dardonne said, "Step, step LEAP, step, step LEAP!" She said it over and over, and still Sam had to think very hard about what to do. She thought, *left, left,* and out of nowhere her right leg appeared, flinging itself out. Her stomach turned. *What was wrong with her?* She knew the steps. But the other bodies—they confused her. They pulled her away from her own thoughts. She wanted the bar, the cool solid roundness underneath, the way it made her palm smell nice, like sweet, salty rust.

Her mother, after lessons, asked to see what Sam had learned. Sam tried hard to remember, standing in the living room, still in her leotard. Her father was there and he pretended not to, but he was watching, and Sam liked that, too. Her mother told her to push her shoulders back and hold her arms in an arc, as though she was hugging a giant ball. Arms were very important. "Make them strong," said her mother. "Then people won't notice your feet so much."

Ms. Dardonne thought Sam might be dyslexic.

"That's ridiculous," said Sam's mother. "You're just not concentrating."

They began to practice before Dad came in, on days when Sam didn't have classes. Mom sipped her Bloody Mary and put on very old records, classical music, and she taught Sam routines she remembered. She taught Sam to make an L with her thumb and forefinger.

"See? L for left." And Sam would make the L automatically, for the rest of her life, whenever anyone asked her for directions.

Sam wasn't dyslexic after all. She was glad, she supposed, but it was a little disappointing. It would have been nice to have a reason.

***

In October, Dad's work days were longer. His boots made heavy sounds against the worn floorboards of the shop. On weekends, Sam wrapped at his worktable and felt the tremors of his steps.

He kept the radio on all day as he drew and cut his patterns. He liked the Eagles and the Steve Miller Band and Jackson Browne. He liked Stevie Nicks but he didn't like Blondie or Pat Benatar.

On his worktable, he kept a notebook, a straight edge ruler, a compass, and a coffee mug of yellow #2 pencils, the erasers nibbled, like a squirrel had been there. He drew and chewed and Sam watched him until he forgot she was there.

A space heater kept the shop warm and three big lamps hung from the ceiling like umbrellas. There was a hot plate and a kettle, for tea breaks, and an old, torn couch in the corner. There were metal shelves stacked high with her father's tools: pattern shears and breaking pliers, X-Acto knives and glass-grinders. There were soldering irons and burnishers to meld the copper foil, and wooden jigs, like frames, for holding the glass pieces together. There was one jagged hacksaw that Sam wasn't allowed to touch.

"DAD."

He looked up, surfacing. He asked if she was bored yet and she said no, not really, and he said didn't she want to play outside? Swing? Hunt for acorns? She said she was too old for that. She kept wrapping.

In November, her father hired a girl named Sharon McDougal, who lived just a few miles away on Red Pine Road. Sharon had been a student at the Portland College of Art and was Dad's helper for the season, or apprentice, as she called herself.

"She's slow," said Sam.

"She's learning," said Dad.

Sharon came to the shop on Saturday afternoons wearing thick wool sweaters patterned in purples and blues. She tied back her long hair with a pewter barrette shaped like a scallop. Her wedding ring had a tiny diamond. She'd married a lobsterman, Sam's father said, when she was just eighteen. The lobsterman's name was Brady and he was a loud, friendly sort with long hair and a boat called *The Sharon Louise*. On weekends, Brady went diving for sea urchins, which was very hard work for good money, because urchins were a delicacy in Japan.

One time, diving, Brady got caught. (Sam's father cleared his throat.) A buoy line, he said.

Sam wanted more, but her father wouldn't say. Brady had gone diving, and he'd died. It was a very dangerous job to have.

Sharon had moved away and tried art school, but she came back after a year. She hadn't cared much for Portland, she told Sam's father.

Late one afternoon, the heater churning, Sam sneaked up behind and released the clasp of Sharon's barrette and watched Sharon's hair fall to her waist.

Sharon whirled around, her loose strands black and soft looking. "Quit it, Sammy." Her face was rattled.

"You—*widow*," said Sam, trying out the word.

Sam spent the rest of the afternoon in the woods behind the house. She'd meant to say: *Only Dad calls me that.*

★★★

On Thanksgiving weekend, Dad's truck, parked along the shore side, was the only car on Ocean Point Road. Sam sat in the truck's cab next to her father with the heat on, rubbing her hands together. The tide was coming in and her father stared; gray waves lapped at the seaweed, covering up the tidal pools. The sun was distant and Arctic looking, a frozen yellow smudge. Rainwater dripped from Sam's red poncho and made the seat damp. Her fingers were gritty with sand.

"Slim pickings today," her father said. He reached across the cab for his tobacco in the glove compartment.

Sam held a blue Tupperware container in her lap. The lid was gone, so her mother let them use it for shells. Today they had ten good mussels, five periwinkles, two razor clams, one dried-out sea urchin, and a black rock with a white ring around it. The rock couldn't be soldered, but her father said she should make a wish and throw it out to sea. Like birthday wishes, he said, like throwing pennies in the fountain at the Portland Mall.

Dumb, Sam thought. *They never come true.*

They were parked across the street from the old stone chapel. It was boarded up now, but from May to September there were weddings there every weekend, mostly for summer people. It was a tiny church, with a single stained glass porthole above the door.

Sam pointed. "Who made that window?"

"Not sure," her father said. He smoked and stared at the waves. After a while he said, "Your mother wanted to get married there, but it was pricey."

"How old were you?"

He looked up, surprised by the question.

"Pretty young."

"As young as Sharon and Brady were?"

He looked down at his fingers, his knuckles red. "Almost." He placed more tobacco in the center of another white square.

Sam waited for him to lick the cigarette shut, then asked, "When Brady drowned, did you go to the funeral?"

"No, I didn't know Sharon then."

"Sharon should've stayed in school, Mom said."

"Did she now." He struck a match.

"Sharon could be an art teacher that way. But then she wouldn't work for you."

"No," her father said. He recognized Davey Johnson's blue Ford Fiesta in the rearview mirror and jerked his head up in greeting. The heat was on full-blast now. Sam held her hands in front of the vent.

"Warming up?" he said.

Sam nodded. She didn't want to leave.

Her father rolled down the window an inch and flicked out the cigarette, then revved the truck's old engine. The lobster buoys bobbed, their white stems all tipped at the same angle, like dancers in a line.

★★★

Sam took ballet on Tuesdays and Thursdays and piano lessons on Fridays. Mr. Hart lived just five houses down the road, but Sam liked to pretend it was much further away, and that wild animals lurked in the ditches.

Mr. Hart had very long fingers and lived alone, except for his Siamese cat, Brava. He made Sam a cup of cocoa and showed her photo albums from when he'd lived in New York and Paris and Berlin. He was thinner in these pictures, and handsome. He was Ms. Dardonne's friend—there were pictures of them together, sipping cocktails at Fisherman's Wharf.

The piano took up Mr. Hart's entire living room. In his kitchen, Mr. Hart had a shelf filled with porcelain figurines. Sam's favorite was a mermaid holding a marble-sized crystal ball in her tiny white hands.

"You'll get it," said Mr. Hart. He meant "Let It Be," which was harder than it sounded. He closed the book and let her take it home. They were ending the lesson early. He had a date with Ms. Dardonne.

Sam walked home as slowly as possible, placing her heel exactly in front of her toe. She held the Beatles book against her chest, careful not to bend the pages. The sky was losing light and the ground was slick with dead, brown leaves. There were slugs underneath, she imagined, orange and fat. The birch trees were bare. It would be nice to peel off the bark in thin white sheets, but it wasn't good for the tree.

She'd have plenty of glass to wrap, with Christmas coming soon. Even her mother had been helping out, letting her tea go cold.

She passed the Kensey's house and counted twenty-two lobster traps stacked on the front lawn. Mrs. Kensey would place a single white candle in each window. Sam's mother would make wreaths from snapped pine boughs and Dad would put one on the shop door. Her mother made blackberry jam at Christmas, too. Maybe she'd made some already. Maybe she and Dad would be in the kitchen when she got home, lips sticky, crumbs on the table.

Sam walked around back first, to the shop. Red pieces today, probably—they'd finished all the green. The pine door was swollen and damp and she had to push hard with her shoulder to open it. The lights were out but the space heater was on, casting an orange shadow on the floorboards. It was very quiet. Something moved in the corner, near the couch. "Dad?" She saw the outline of her father's boots near the heater and something fuzzy and soft on the worktable, a sweater.

"Sam. Go back in the house." Dad's voice was cool, stern. Sam didn't move, didn't even exhale.

"Get out, Sam. *Now*."

She ran, her feet heavy. She dropped the Beatles book and picked it up, brushing away damp leaves. Outside everything was in shadow, except one thick streak of sky, all fiery and rust-colored, huge and angry and much too far away.

***

Years later, when Sam thought of that day, she pictured Sharon and her father on the kitchen table, jam on Sharon's lips and Dad's hands clutching at her. There was jam everywhere, everything sticky.

At the time, she had a sharp feeling in her gut, like glass inside. She tried hard to imagine nothing. She said nothing.

Her mother found out anyway. From her room Sam heard a short laugh like a bark, like something was caught in her mother's throat. Then her father slammed doors (house, porch, pickup). He didn't go anywhere, just sat in the truck smoking for an hour, then two, flicking out the rolled butts until there was a little pile under the driver's window.

A week later, her mother put her vanity case and a duffel bag in the back of the old Subaru and drove all the way to Key West, where the highway stopped. She worked at a bar called Lucky's where she had to wear a purple tank top, she wrote. She sent postcards of pelicans, of Ernest Hemingway's house. Her bank uniform hung in the closet, pressed and starched.

Sam stayed in her room and traced her finger along I-95 in her father's atlas, Maine to Florida. It was nothing, just three finger-lengths down the page.

Sharon was gone. She went back to school. This is what Allie Thompson told Sam. Allie was Sam's best friend, and Allie's mother got her hair cut by Sharon's mother, and this is what Mrs. Thompson heard during her tri-monthly perm and set.

***

By March, the birch trees had tiny buds and Sam's shoes were muddy. Her mother called and asked if she'd like to spend the summer in Florida. Her voice sounded different, the tightness in her throat gone. She sounded tan and pretty.

"I have my lessons," said Sam. "My recital." *Come get me*, she thought. She felt a tug like a rope tightening.

Sam practiced the Beatles songs in her room, on the paper keyboard on the back cover of the Young Adult Piano Book #1. She tried to hear the notes in her head and sometimes this kept her from hearing the TV downstairs and her father coughing in front of it. She made up songs of her own. She did pliés in front of the mirror, in her tiara. She was too old for the tiara, but she wanted to wear it still.

She thought of Sharon's finger, on the left hand, with the tiny diamond.

She thought of Key West as a steep green cliff and her mother standing too close to the edge.

She practiced.

***

In the fall, Sam was allowed to start jazz classes at the Brunswick Y, forty minutes away, and by the time they got back to town the roads were black and empty. Dad drove fast, with the stereo on, the window wide open. He smoked and didn't sing. He'd stopped rolling cigarettes. He bought Marlboro Reds instead.

Sam was the youngest one in the class. Ms. Lynn, the teacher, said, "You have grace. It's a gift."

"It's from my mother," said Sam, and handed over the checks.

Ms. Lynn wanted Sam to take a modern class, too, but her father wouldn't budge.

He spent more time in the shop, alone. The house smelled musty, like wet leaves. Sam lit all the candles at once: Apple Cinnamon, Vanilla Musk, Lilac Breeze. She watched them burn and puddle, waiting for her tea to cool.

***

For Halloween, Sam was John and Allie was Paul. Allie took lessons from Mr. Hart, too. She was already on book #3, and she had a two-octave Casio to practice on, with drum beats: salsa, march, waltz, and rock. She wanted Sam to spend the monthly checks on 45s, but Sam wouldn't. Allie had a big 45 collection already, alphabetized by artist.

Sam's mom sent a postcard of a Carnival ship, docked in Miami. She said she'd been on a mini-cruise to the Bahamas, with a friend. The ship was very large, like a perfect tooth. The dancers wore feathers and rhinestone earrings, she wrote.

Sam would never work in a bank or a bar, she decided, and she wouldn't sit in a dark shop and make things all day. *Solid Gold* had gone off the air, but she had a new plan. She would be a Radio City Rockette. She would have to be five-foot-five, at least. Allie was the only one she told.

"You probably won't be tall enough," Allie said.

Allie was going to be a keyboard player for Prince.

"He plays the piano himself," Sam pointed out.

"I'll do it for him. He'll be free to sing and dance that way."

They would be famous, this was certain. They just had to get out.

***

Her mother flew back to Maine for a visit after Thanksgiving. She took Sam to the Tugboat Inn and ordered ginger ales for both of them. Her hair was shorter and she wore a bracelet with small coral hearts. She asked about Sam's dance classes and showed pictures from her Bahamas trip.

Sam slid her orange garnish from the side of her glass and chewed. "You know the *Chorus Line* story?" Sam said. Her heart rattled but she couldn't stop herself. "It sounds made up."

"It's not made up," said Sam's mother. She sucked the last of her ginger ale.

In the harbor the water was steely and quiet. No waves. Sam waited, but her mother just smiled hard. Then she asked for the bill.

***

The piano recital was a week before Christmas and Sam only made one flub. Ms. Dardonne came and sat in the front row. Her father came and clapped too much. Allie went last and played "Long and Winding Road."

Sam began to have the same dream. The ship's funnel was spewing brown leaves, thousands of them, so many that the green Astroturf of the deck was covered, and stems were caught in the plastic slats of sun chairs. Sam knew the shape of the leaves but couldn't remember the tree name. And she knew her father was there—underneath somewhere, hiding.

Her mother was there too, standing at the ship's rail with her new haircut ruffled. The leaves swirled around her and the sea churned below, and her mother just kept standing there on deck, as if she'd taken root. She clenched something in her fist. And when she saw Sam, she sprung into action, beautifully. She twirled and arched, and flung back her rigid arm like a pitcher, like an expert. She threw just as far as she could.

"Glass" is from Lara Tupper's short story collection, Amphibians, *winner of the Leapfrog Press Global Fiction Prize and published by Leapfrog Press in 2021.*

About the Contributors

Shannon Bowring's work has appeared in numerous journals and has been nominated for Pushcart and Best of the Net prizes. She has been recognized on such short- and long-lists as the Maine Literary Awards and the *Writer's Digest* Short Story Competition. Her debut novel, *The Road to Dalton*, was included in the June 2023 Indie Next List and chosen as one of NPR's Books We Love in 2023. The sequel to *Dalton*, *Where the Forest Meets the River*, is forthcoming from Europa Editions. Shannon earned her MFA in Creative Writing from Stonecoast at the University of Southern Maine. Raised up in The County (if you know, you know), she now resides in the mid-coast region of Maine, where she works as a cataloger at her local library. When she's not writing, Shannon enjoys reading, baking, and spending time with her husband and nearly-toothless cat.

Paul Carro is an active Horror Writers Association member and author of the acclaimed horror novels *The House* and *Abject Fear*. His short stories have appeared in multiple anthologies, and he edits *The Little Coffee Shop of Horrors* anthologies. His screenplay *Penance* is set up with legendary film producer

Michael Phillips. He is also in development on *Hitchcock, Nebraska* as writer/producer with horror flick director Rolfe Kanefsky attached to direct. Paul has served as a producer/writer in film and reality TV, and he resides in Santa Monica, California.

Charlotte Crowder lives and writes on the coast of Maine. An accredited editor in the life sciences, she is a medical writer and editor with a master's degree in public health. Her publications include, among others, short stories in *Tamarind Magazine, Present Tense, Intima, Branching Out: International Tales of Brilliant Flash Fiction, American Writers Review,* and a picture book, *A Fine Orange Bucket* (North Country Press, 2019).

Cynthia Graae lives in New York City and Hiram, Maine. She writes short fiction and autobiographical nonfiction. Her stories about her late husband, including the sequel to "Seeing the Light," payback for his stunts (*The Common Dispatches*), a holdup at gunpoint (*Humans in the Wild,* a Swallow Press anthology about gun violence), marital disputes (*Exsolutas Press, Griffel,* and *10x10 Flash*), protesting the Vietnam War (*Courageous Conversations on Maine Public*), a how-we-met, on a North Sea ferry (*The Bridge: Journal of the Danish American Society*), and a mysterious happening the night before his death (*Deep Overstock,* the ghost issue). Cynthia enjoys concerts, theater, opera, hanging out with friends and family, and being outdoors. When she isn't writing, she seeks homes for her unpublished stories; there are many more about her late husband.

Emily Knowles aka Emma Wilde splits her time between creating digital art—like the piece that graces the cover of this anthology—and crafting romance novellas and TV scripts. Her artwork features brightly colored land and seascapes and has been published in *Archetype* and *Beyond Words Literary Magazine*. Much of her work featuring sunsets, ocean waves, and mountains hangs in homes around the world. Emily is an award-winning author and has been published in *The Washington Post* among other places. She's a native Mainer but currently resides in southwest Louisiana, where she draws on a whole new landscape. You can see and read more of her work at emilyknowles-artist.com.

Karen Menzel (née Bovenmyer) earned an MFA in Creative Writing, Popular Fiction from the University of Southern Maine. She teaches and mentors students at Iowa State University. She has served as the assistant editor of the *Pseudopod Horror Podcast Magazine*. She is the 2016 recipient of the Horror Writers Association Mary Wollstonecraft Shelley Scholarship. Her poems, short stories, and novellas appear in more than 40 publications and her first novel, *Swift for the Sun*, debuted from Dreamspinner Press in 2017.

Sarah Parke holds an MFA in Popular Fiction from the University of Southern Maine's Stonecoast MFA program. She has been published in *The Writer* and *Speculative City*, and her fiction plays with alternate historic timelines and magical circumstances. Earlier in her own timeline, she spent six years helping authors polish their prose as an acquiring editor at a regional trade publisher. She currently works at Wesleyan University where she writes stories about the campus community for the magazine and newsletter. A New England native, Sarah lives in Connecticut with her husband, Sean.

Mary E. Plouffe is a clinical psychologist and author of *I Know It in My Heart: Walking Through Grief with a Child* (She Writes Press, 2017), a memoir finalist in the Maine Literary Awards, and winner of the Independent Publishers of New England's 2018 Book of the Year. She writes essays, flash fiction, and opinion pieces that view the world through a psychological lens. Recent essays have appeared in the anthologies *Breaking Bread* (Beacon, 2022) and *Art in a Time of Unbearable Crisis* (She Writes Press, 2022). Full publication history can be found at maryeplouffeauthor.com. She lives and works in beautiful southern Maine.

Bruce Pratt is an award-winning novelist, short story writer, poet, and playwright. He is the author of the novel *The Serpents of Blissfull* (Mountain State Press, 2011), the poetry collection *Boreal* (Antrim House, 2007), *The Trash Detail: Stories* (New Rivers Press, 2018), and the poetry chapbook *Forms and Shades* (Clare Songbirds Publishing, 2019). His fiction, poetry, drama, and essays have appeared in more than 50 magazines, reviews, and journals across the United States, Canada, Ireland, and Wales. He is the editor of *American Fiction*.

On a western Wyoming homestead, **sid sibo** feeds thin mountain soil and tends a mixed community of plants and critters. Story seeds sprout here in lush mounds of manure, and their fruits include a number of flash pieces and short stories in places like *Orca, Cutthroat, The Hopper, Cardinal Sins*, and *Fourth River*, along with a novel under contract for 2024 publication. Early life, and a much later MFA, grew on Maine's cool ledgerock. Find more at the Acoustic Burro blog, sibomountain.net.

A graduate of USM's Stonecoast MFA program as a student of fiction, **Michelle Soucy's** work has appeared in various journals such as *The Florida Review, The Bryant Literary Review, EWR: Stories*, and others. Her creative nonfiction was also included in the anthology, *Idol Talk: Women Writers on the Teenage Infatuations That Changed Their Lives (McFarland & Company, 2018)*. In the past she was on the editorial staff of literary journals, newspapers, and magazines, and has taught various writing workshops and seminars. Michelle was born in Maine; her family moved to Florida when she was nine. She returned to New England as an adult and now lives in Massachusetts with her husband and cat, along with many birds and wildlife along the Still River. In 1948, her grandfather purchased land all along a large pond in Hancock County, Maine—depicted in the poem in this anthology—where her family continues to share many golden sunshine and moon-lit adventures.

Clif Travers is a visual artist and writer living in Portland, Maine. His writing has been featured in *Underwood Press, Freeze Frame Fiction, Coffin Bell Journal, Crack the Spine Anthology, Dime Show Review*, and *Sonora Review*, among others. His collection of linked stories, *The Stones of Riverton*, was published by Down East Books in September of 2023. Clif received his MFA in creative writing from Stonecoast at the University of Southern Maine, and he teaches creative writing at Writerfest in New York, The Writing Center in Gloucester Massachusetts, the MWPA in Portland, Maine, and Maine Media in Camden, Maine.

Lara Tupper is the author of three books: *Amphibians* (Leapfrog Press, 2021), a story collection which won the Leapfrog Global Fiction Prize; *Off Island: A Novel* (Encircle Publications, 2020), finalist for the Housatonic Book Award; and the novel *A Thousand and One Nights* (Untreed Reads, 2015). She recently received a Martha Boschen Porter Fund Award for Writers and was a finalist for the Nicholas Schaffner Award for Music in Literature, the Orison Fiction Prize, and the UNO Publishing Lab Prize. A graduate of the MFA Program for Writers at Warren Wilson College, she taught creative writing for many years at Rutgers University and is founder of Swift Ink Stories, a platform for workshops and manuscript development. Lara is also a jazz/folk performer who has traveled the world. She is proud to be from Maine. For more information, visit laratupper.com or follow @laratupper.

About the Publisher

Rogue Owl Press is an independent publisher specializing in *startling stories*. We're drawn to writing that is entertaining, exciting, and captivating, while simultaneously powerful, complex, and genre-bending.

Writing may be considered startling for many reasons. Startling stories transcend any one genre, style, or storytelling philosophy. A startling piece of writing may work within genre conventions or defy expectations altogether. But such works all have one thing in common: their beating hearts. Startling stories are alive.

We publish writing that stops us, as readers, in our tracks and jolts us in astonishing ways. We seek creative work that makes us ponder the universe from a new angle and provides an opening to fall into another reality. In the words of Jack Kerouac, we want to feel everything all at once.

Find more startling stories at **www.rogueowlpress.com/join**.